**The outstanding new thriller from #1 *New York Times*–bestselling author Stuart Woods.**

Stone Barrington isn't one to turn away in the face of danger, so when he witnesses a tricky situation under way, he jumps in to lend a hand. He never expected, though, that this favor would lead to a mutually beneficial business deal with a prominent gentleman who requires the ever discreet services of Woodman & Weld.

But in the ruthless corporate world no good deed goes unpunished, and Stone soon finds himself the target of a ragtag group of criminal toughs who don't appreciate his interference in their dealings. From the isolated landscape of Maine to the white sand beaches of Key West, the trail of deception, theft, and murder will lead to a perilous confrontation.

## PRAISE FOR THE STONE BARRINGTON NOVELS BY STUART WOODS

### *Foreign Affairs*

"Appealing . . . boasts Woods's customary combination of panache and brio." —*Publishers Weekly*

### *Hot Pursuit*

"Fans will enjoy the vicarious luxury ride." —*Publishers Weekly*

### Doing Hard Time

"High escapist suspense." —*Mystery Scene*

### Unintended Consequences

"Avid fans will enjoy the character's trademark casual, cool demeanor." —*Library Journal*

### Collateral Damage

"High-octane . . . Woods's blend of exciting action, sophisticated gadgetry, and last-minute heroics doesn't disappoint." —*Publishers Weekly*

### Severe Clear

"Stuart Woods has proven time and time again that he's a master of suspense who keeps his readers frantically turning the pages." —Bookreporter.com

### Unnatural Acts

"[It] makes you covet the fast-paced, charmed life of Woods's characters from the safety of your favorite chair." —Code451.com

### D.C. Dead

"Engaging . . . The story line is fast-paced." —*Midwest Book Review*

### Son of Stone

"Woods's vast and loyal audience will be thrilled with a second-generation Barrington charmer."     —*Booklist*

### Bel-Air Dead

"A fast-paced mystery with an inside look into Hollywood and the motion picture business. Barrington fans will enjoy it."     —*The Oklahoman*

### Strategic Moves

"The action never slows from the start."
                                        —*Midwest Book Review*

### Lucid Intervals

"Woods mixes danger and humor into a racy concoction that will leave readers thirsty for more."
                                        —*Publishers Weekly*

### Kisser

"POW!!! He's back with more twists and trysts."
                                        —The Mystery Reader

# BOOKS BY STUART WOODS

## FICTION

*Family Jewels*[†]
*Scandalous Behavior*[†]
*Foreign Affairs*[†]
*Naked Greed*[†]
*Hot Pursuit*[†]
*Insatiable Appetites*[†]
*Paris Match*[†]
*Cut and Thrust*[†]
*Carnal Curiosity*[†]
*Standup Guy*[†]
*Doing Hard Time*[†]
*Unintended Consequences*[†]
*Collateral Damage*[†]
*Severe Clear*[†]
*Unnatural Acts*[†]
*D.C. Dead*[†]
*Son of Stone*[†]
*Bel-Air Dead*[†]
*Strategic Moves*[†]
*Santa Fe Edge*[§]
*Lucid Intervals*[†]

*Kisser*[†]
*Hothouse Orchid*[*]
*Loitering with Intent*[†]
*Mounting Fears*[†]
*Hot Mahogany*[†]
*Santa Fe Dead*[§]
*Beverly Hills Dead*
*Shoot Him If He Runs*[†]
*Fresh Disasters*[†]
*Short Straw*[§]
*Dark Harbor*[†]
*Iron Orchid*[*]
*Two Dollar Bill*[†]
*The Prince of Beverly Hills*
*Reckless Abandon*[†]
*Capital Crimes*[‡]
*Dirty Work*[†]
*Blood Orchid*[*]
*The Short Forever*[†]
*Orchid Blues*[*]
*Cold Paradise*[†]

*L.A. Dead*[†]
*The Run*[‡]
*Worst Fears Realized*[†]
*Orchid Beach*[*]
*Swimming to Catalina*[†]
*Dead in the Water*[†]
*Dirt*[†]
*Choke*
*Imperfect Strangers*
*Heat*
*Dead Eyes*
*L.A. Times*
*Santa Fe Rules*[§]
*New York Dead*[†]
*Palindrome*
*Grass Roots*[‡]
*White Cargo*
*Under the Lake*
*Deep Lie*[‡]
*Run Before the Wind*[‡]
*Chiefs*[‡]

## TRAVEL

*A Romantic's Guide to the Country Inns of Britain and Ireland* (1979)

## MEMOIR

*Blue Water, Green Skipper*

[*] *A Holly Barker Novel*
[†] *A Stone Barrington Novel*
[‡] *A Will Lee Novel*
[§] *An Ed Eagle Novel*

# STUART WOODS

G. P. PUTNAM'S SONS  *New York*

G. P. PUTNAM'S SONS
*Publishers Since 1838*
An imprint of Penguin Random House LLC
375 Hudson Street
New York, New York 10014

First G. P. Putnam's Sons hardcover edition / October 2015
G. P. Putnam's Sons premium edition / June 2016
G. P. Putnam's Sons premium edition ISBN: 978-0-451-47722-4

Printed in the United States of America
1  3  5  7  9  10  8  6  4  2

Book design by Nicole Laroche

# FOREIGN *Affairs*

# I

S tone Barrington was at dinner at Patroon, a favorite restaurant, with Dino and Viv Bacchetti, his closest friends.

"Stone," Viv said, "don't you sometimes wish you were still a cop?" Stone had spent fourteen years on the NYPD, most of them as a homicide detective with Dino as his partner.

"Viv," Stone replied, "with the kindest possible intention, are you out of your fucking mind?"

Viv burst out laughing.

Dino looked at him with pity. "He wishes he was still a cop every time I tell him about something the department is investigating."

"The only time I wish I were a cop," Stone said, "is when somebody is double-parked in front of my house and I'm having trouble getting the car out of the garage."

"You mean, you want to arrest the driver?" Viv asked.

"No, I want to shoot him."

"Stone thinks the worst crime we have to deal with is double-parking in his block," Dino pointed out.

"No, I just think it's the worst crime within gun-shot range of my garage door."

"That seems a drastic remedy," Viv said.

"Not when you consider that I'd only have to do it once—word would get around, then nobody would double-park in front of my house."

"It wouldn't matter, because you'd be in jail for quite a long time," Dino said.

"You mean, you'd have me arrested for shooting a double-parker?" Dino had stayed on the NYPD and was now police commissioner of New York.

"Of course. You'd get no special treatment."

"I didn't mean I'd kill the guy, just shoot him a little."

"Then you'd spend less time in jail. With good behavior you'd be out in seven to ten."

"But I still have a badge."

"Take a close look at your solid-gold, honorary-detective-first-class badge that was given to you by our former commissioner, now mayor. It's not engraved with the words 'Authorized to shoot anybody who annoys him.'"

"Not even double-parkers who block my garage door?"

"Especially not them."

Stone's cell phone rang and he looked at the number. "It's Joan," he said. "She never calls at this time of night. I'd better get it. Hello?"

"It's Joan."

"I know, I have caller ID."

"I've made a tiny little mistake," she said.

"Oh, God," Stone moaned. He covered the phone. "Joan says she's made a tiny little mistake," he said to his companions. "That means she's made a real whopper of a mistake." He went back to the phone. "All right, let me have it."

"There's good news and bad news," she said. "The good news is that I forgot to put a board meeting of the Arrington Group on your calendar."

Stone was immediately suspicious. "And what is the bad news?"

"The meeting is tomorrow," she said. "At noon."

"Well, I can probably get out of bed early enough to make that."

"That's not all the bad news."

"Oh, God," Stone said, mostly to himself.

"You already said that."

"What's the rest of the bad news?"

"The board meeting is in Rome."

"Rome is up the Hudson somewhere, isn't it?"

"Not that Rome."

"Rome, Georgia? Rome has an airport. I could fly myself down there tomorrow morning."

"Think farther east."

"Oh, God," Stone said. "Not *that* Rome."

"That one. Now don't say, 'Oh, God' again, and don't panic—there's an Alitalia flight tonight."

"What time?"

"In, let's see, fifty-four minutes."

"Which airport?"

"JFK."

"That's a forty-five-minute drive," he pointed out.

"And Fred is off tonight, he went to the theater."

"I'll never make it," he said.

"Think about this: you're sitting next to the guy with the fastest car in town."

"Hang on a minute." He turned to Dino. "I've got to be at JFK in fifty-four minutes to catch a plane to Rome. Can I borrow your car?"

"You mean the one with the flashing lights on top?"

"That's the one."

"I can see the headlines in tomorrow's *Post*," Dino

said. "POLICE COMMISH LOANS OFFICIAL CAR TO SCHMUCK, WHO IS INVOLVED IN TERRIBLE ACCIDENT."

"Fifty-three minutes!" Joan shouted from the other end of the phone call.

"Only if I'm in the car with you," Dino said. "That would shorten the headline to, SCHMUCK HITCHES RIDE WITH COMMISH."

"You two better get going," Viv said.

"You're not coming with us?" Stone asked.

"I'd scream all the way," she replied. "Go on, get your asses in gear! I'll get the check."

"I'll call you en route with further instructions," he said to Joan, then hung up and ran for the door, followed closely by Dino.

# 2

D ino got into the backseat of the black SUV with Stone and slammed the door. "We've got fifty-one minutes to make a flight at JFK," he said to his driver. "Punch it, and use the siren and the lights."

"God bless you," Stone said, patting him on the knee.

"Don't bring God into this, and don't put your hand on my knee."

"You want me to shoot him, boss?" the detective in the front passenger seat asked.

"Not unless he does it again. You get on the horn to security at Kennedy and tell them I want to drive onto the ramp. Find out what gate the Alitalia flight to Rome is occupying, and tell them to stand by for an arriving passenger, Barrington."

"Yes, sir." The detective whipped out his phone. Stone dialed Joan's number.

"I'm here."

"Am I on the flight?" he shouted over the siren.

"You are—you got the last seat, and I ordered you a car."

"Good. I need a room at the Hassler in Rome."

"I've already called them and talked to the night man. It's the middle of the night there, but he's promised to have you a bed, he just can't promise you a suite."

"Where's the board meeting tomorrow?"

"In a conference room at the Hassler."

"When did we get notice of the meeting?"

"Do you really need to know?"

"Yes, I do."

"Maybe ten days ago. I got busy and . . ."

"Okay, go upstairs to my dressing room and pack the following, ready?"

"Shoot."

"Use the two medium-sized cases. Pack a blue suit, a chalk-stripe, and—I don't know, maybe a tuxedo, pleated shirt, and black tie. Pack the black alligator oxfords, six pairs of boxers, six pairs of black socks, half a dozen linen handkerchiefs, and six shirts that go with the suits and half a dozen ties, and include my travel toiletries kit. Oh, shit, I don't have my passport. Find it."

"Are you wearing your blue blazer with the yacht club buttons?"

"Yes."

"Try the left inside pocket."

Stone slapped his chest, rummaged in the pocket, and came up with the alligator passport case. "Got it. How did you know where it was?"

"When the new one came in the mail, I saw you put it there. What else do you need?"

"A briefcase—the black alligator one, and all the stuff that's in it. You might make sure there's a legal pad in there."

"Right. What else?"

"Is it cold in Rome?"

"It's spring, and Rome is a subtropical climate."

"No coat, then. What's the agenda for the board meeting?"

"I'll fax it to you before I go to bed."

"FedEx the luggage, so it'll be there the day after tomorrow. I'll make do until then."

"Have a good trip."

"Bye." Stone hung up and looked around. They were on what looked like the Van Wyck Expressway, and cars were scattering before them. "I like this," he said. "This is how to go to the airport."

"You're lucky it isn't rush hour," the driver said.

"He's lucky he knows me," Dino said.

"I know you, and I love you, Dino."

"Stop that."

"Is his hand on your knee again, boss?" the detective asked.

"He knows better than that now."

"Shucks, I was counting on shooting him."

They were off the expressway and onto the labyrinth of roads around the airport. They stopped at a gate, which rolled back to admit them, and a security guard gave them the gate number and directions.

"You can turn off the siren now," Dino said. "But keep the lights on."

"Gotcha, boss." The driver floored it, and two minutes later they pulled up next to a giant airplane, connected to the terminal by a snaking boarding tunnel.

"Thanks, Dino," Stone said. "I owe you."

"I'll send you a bill. Now get your ass on the plane—it was supposed to push back three minutes ago."

A security guard waved Stone to a door, and he ran up a flight of stairs, emerging in the tunnel near the aircraft door. A flight attendant awaited, his hand on the door. "Any luggage, Mr. Barrington?"

"None," Stone said, entering the airplane.

"Just a moment." He closed the door behind them, turned right, and started down an aisle. They were in the tourist cabin, and the attendant was pointing at a seat right in the middle of the airplane.

"Wait a minute—no first class?" Stone asked.

"The flight is full. This is it."

Stone sighed and squeezed past the knees of two very large passengers and flopped into the seat. An extremely fat man sat to his left, taking up the entire armrest. "Welcome aboard," he said.

"Thanks." Stone looked to his right and found a woman of reasonable proportions.

"Aren't you the lucky guy?" she said.

"Not lucky enough," Stone said, trying to find something to do with his left arm. "How long is this flight?"

"For me, nine hours. For you, forever."

"Too right."

"I'm Hedy Kiesler," she said. "Actually Hedwig Eva Maria Kiesler, but only my mother calls me that."

"All of it?"

"Just Hedwig. If you call me anything but Hedy, I'll hurt you."

"I believe you," Stone said, offering a hand. "I'm Stone Barrington."

She leaned in. "I'm glad you made it. I thought I was going to have to deal with the fat guy."

"I heard that!" the fat guy said.

"Sorry."

The airplane was moving backward; after a moment an engine started. A female flight attendant appeared. "Mr. Barrington? I have two seats for you and your companion in first class."

"What companion?" Hedy asked Stone.

"I think she means you. Join me?"

"You bet your sweet ass," she said.

The two of them struggled past the two fat men. "Good riddance," one of them said. "Move over one, George."

Stone, followed by Hedy, walked up the aisle and was shown to the first pair of seats at the front of the cabin. "You can have the window," he said.

"I'm sorry we couldn't seat you sooner," the attendant said, "but the seats were booked by someone else who didn't show. I had to wait until we closed the door and pushed back before giving them to you."

Hedy eased into her seat. "God, what a relief," she said. "Do you always fly like this?"

"No, usually I fly myself in a light jet."

"Why not tonight?"

"I had to leave on short notice for a board meeting tomorrow in Rome."

"What kind of board?"

"A hotel group. What takes you to Rome?"

"I'm a painter. I've taken an apartment for a month, and I'm going to paint Rome."

"I don't see any canvases or paints."

"I shipped all that ahead."

"Where's your apartment?"

"In the Pantheon district."

"Nice."

"Where are you staying?"

"At the Hassler Villa Medici."

"*Very* nice."

The airplane rolled onto the runway and accelerated. Shortly, the attendant brought them dinner menus.

"I'm starved," Hedy said, opening the menu. "How about you?"

"I had a first course before my secretary called and told me I had to go to Rome."

"No luggage?"

"Not even a briefcase. I was lucky my passport was in my jacket pocket. Can I buy you a drink?"

"Several," she said. "I'm terrified of flying."

"You don't look terrified."

"I guess you're a calming influence," she said. "I know bourbon is."

Stone ordered two double bourbons.

# 3

The cabin lights came on, and a voice blared over the loudspeakers, first in Italian, then: "Ladies and gentlemen, we will land in Rome in approximately one hour. Breakfast will now be served."

Stone realized there was a head on his shoulder. She made a noise and sat up. "Did she say breakfast?"

"We ordered it last night, don't you remember?"

"I remember only bourbon, but I don't remember how many."

"Don't ask."

A flight attendant set omelets before them and they ate hungrily.

"How do you feel?" Stone asked when their plates had been taken away.

"Nearly human."

\*　　\*　　\*

They deplaned and walked toward baggage claim. She was pulling a carry-on.

"Do you have any checked luggage?" Stone asked.

"No, I sent it with the painting stuff."

"Smart. Can I give you a lift into the city?"

"Sure."

They walked through customs without incident, and Stone saw a man holding a sign with his name on it. A couple of minutes later they were in a large Mercedes sedan.

"You travel well," she said. "What do you do?"

"I'm an attorney."

"What firm?"

"Woodman & Weld."

"They represent my stepfather," she said.

"Who's your stepfather?"

"His name is Arthur Steele."

"I'm his lawyer. I represent the Steele insurance group."

"I believe this is where I say, 'Small world.'"

"Not yet—my mother was a painter."

"What was her name?"

"Matilda Stone. Now you can say it."

"Small world. I know her stuff from the American Collection at the Metropolitan."

"Come over to my house when you get back to New York, and I'll show you another dozen."

"Beats etchings." She got out her phone and made a call, then hung up. "Shit."

"What's the matter?"

"My apartment rental doesn't start until the day after tomorrow. They had told me I could probably get in a couple of days early, but nooooo."

"I'll put you up at the Hassler, if you like. I don't know what kind of accommodations I have yet, but there's probably a sofa."

"For me or for you?"

"For you."

"Well, I guess if you're my stepfather's lawyer you can't do anything terrible to me."

"I think that was part of my oath. I can't do anything terrible to a client's daughter."

"You're on."

An hour later, after fighting Roman rush hour traffic, they pulled up in front of the Hassler. Stone presented himself at the front desk.

"Good morning, Mr. Barrington. We got your call last night, and we've given you the only suite left in the hotel. Do you have any luggage?"

"Just the lady's," Stone said, indicating his companion. "My luggage won't be here until tomorrow. Do you think your concierge can find me a pair of boxer shorts, size 36, a pair of black socks, and a white shirt, size 16-35?"

"Certainly, sir. There's a shop in the hotel, and if they don't have your sizes, I'll send a boy down into the Via Condotti, where there are many shops. Let me show you to your suite."

The man led them to an elevator and to the top floor. He used a key in a door and ushered them into an enormous living room.

"Are you sure this is all you have left?" Stone asked.

"This is our Presidential Suite San Pietro. It's inadequate, I know, but I'm afraid it's the best we can offer. We're booked up for another ten days."

"Well, I'll just have to make do, I guess."

"Look," Hedy said, "there's a second bedroom—my virtue is safe!"

The man handed over a key. "Is there anything else I can do for you?"

"I'd like to have my clothes pressed, my laundry done, and my shoes polished. I have a board meeting at noon."

"Certainly. I'll send up the valet." He departed, a fifty-dollar bill in his pocket.

"I've got to find a cash machine and get some euros," Stone said, half to himself. "Excuse me, I have to get out of these clothes."

"Already?" Hedy asked. "And I thought my virtue was safe."

Stone found a robe in his bathroom and stripped off everything. When he got back to the living room the doorbell was ringing. He gave his clothes to the valet, with instructions to press his suit, shine his shoes, and launder his other things.

The man accepted the clothes and handed him a shopping bag. "See if these things are satisfactory," he said.

Stone inspected the contents. "Perfect." He sent the man off with another of his fifties.

Hedy had emerged from her bedroom in her own robe. "You overtip."

"Haven't you ever heard of Ronald Reagan's trickledown theory?"

"Yes, I've just never seen it in operation. If you'll excuse me, I'd like to get some sleep in a real bed."

"Of course. Would you like to have dinner with me this evening?"

"I can refuse you nothing," she said, closing the door behind her.

"We'll see," Stone called after her.

The doorbell rang again, and an envelope was slid under the door. Stone opened it to find the agenda for his board meeting. There was only one item: "Consideration of a potential site for a new Arrington Hotel in Rome." It was the first he'd heard of it.

He went to his own bedroom and left a wakeup call for eleven AM. He had two hours to sleep, and he wasted no time becoming unconscious.

# 4

Stone swam up out of a sound sleep and wondered where he was and what that unfamiliar sound meant. He followed it to a telephone. "Yes?" he croaked.

"Your eleven o'clock call, Mr. Barrington."

"Thank you." He hung up and stared at the ceiling until his eyes were fully focused, then he got up and went into the large bathroom. Several toiletry items had been laid out, and he managed a shave followed by a shower that fully woke him. He went back to his room and changed into his new underwear, socks, and shirt, tied his tie, and slipped into his freshly pressed clothes. Quite presentable, he thought, gazing into the mirror.

He went into the living room and saw it as if for the first time: beautiful paneling, exquisite fabrics, and a large painting over the sofa. He walked out onto his terrace and got the full effect of the Roman sunshine and spring air, then he went and sat at his desk, forgetting for a moment that his briefcase and laptop were en route. He took his iPhone off the hotel's charger and checked his e-mail. One from Dino.

*I hope the service was as good in Rome as it was in New York.*

*Not nearly as good*, Stone replied, *and I thank you again.*

The others could wait.

Hedy's bedroom door was ajar; he peeked inside, and saw only a large lump in the bed. He closed it and left the suite, putting the DO NOT DISTURB sign on the doorknob.

He walked down the hall, found the meeting room, and walked in. Half a dozen men and two women were seated around the conference table. The man at the head of the table, his friend Marcel duBois, rose to greet him.

"Ah, Stone, I'm so glad you could make it on such short notice."

"You have no idea," Stone said, embracing him.

"Please have a seat," he said, indicating a chair next to his, "and we will start."

Stone sat down.

"Our purpose for being here," Marcel said, "is to discuss and inspect a potential site for an Arrington Hotel in Rome." He stood and flipped back a page on an easel to reveal a map of Rome. "This," he said, pointing to a red dot, "is the Hassler Villa Medici. This," he said, pointing to a blue dot a short distance away, "is our site. Just the other side of the church next door, on the edge of the Borghese Gardens."

There was a murmur of approval from the group.

"Marcel," a woman said, "how on earth did you manage such a site?"

"Approval had been given to another hotel group to build there, but there were difficulties that could not be resolved. We have the opportunity to buy a hundred-year lease on the land, and there is already planning approval, in principle, for a hotel of two hundred rooms and eight stories."

"What difficulties?" someone asked. "Why would any self-respecting group let go of such a property?"

"You will recall that, until recently, we were in a terrible recession, and Europe has not recovered nearly so quickly as the United States. At a time when others are retrenching, the Arrington Group has the resources to invest."

Stone knew that the resources mentioned were Marcel's, inherited from his father and greatly increased by the son, and his own, inherited from his late wife, Arrington Calder Barrington, and her late husband, the film star Vance Calder, and swollen by a burgeoning stock market.

Marcel mentioned the price.

"Move to buy it," Stone said reflexively.

"Second," someone called out.

"Yea," everyone else shouted.

"Well, ladies and gentlemen," Marcel said, "you have made my job easy. Shall we adjourn to the site and inspect it?"

Ten minutes and a short walk later they were surveying the view over Rome from the hilltop of the Borghese Gardens.

"You will have to imagine, ladies and gentlemen," Marcel said, "the view from our rooftop restaurant, which will be as good as that of the Hassler."

Everyone turned and looked at the half-built skeleton of the abandoned project.

"Our architects tell me that we can utilize all of the previous structure, with some judicious additions."

"Marcel, this is brilliant," someone said.

"Thank you so much. Now shall we adjourn to the Hassler for some lunch?"

The group returned to the hotel, where a convivial luncheon ran on until mid-afternoon.

As the party broke up, Stone pulled Marcel aside. "You mentioned that the previous group had 'difficulties.' What were they?"

"Financial, mostly," Marcel said, avoiding Stone's eye.

"And what are you not telling me?"

"I can tell you that those difficulties have been resolved as a result of our purchase. Now all that remains is for each of us to deposit a very large sum of cash in the Arrington account, and we're off." He handed Stone a letter that was a formal request for Stone's investment.

Stone looked at his watch. "It's early in New York. Is today soon enough?"

Marcel squeezed his arm. "I knew I could rely on your support, my good friend."

S tone returned to his suite, faxed the letter to Joan with an approval to transfer the money, then found Hedy camped on the living room sofa, drinking coffee. "I'm glad to see you awake," he said, joining her and pouring himself some coffee.

"Awake is too strong a word, but the coffee is helping," she replied. "How did your board meeting go?"

"Swimmingly. We approved the purchase of a property quite near here for the construction of a new Arrington."

"I've visited the Arrington in L.A., but not the one in Paris. Will the new Rome Arrington meet their standards?"

"We have a Frenchman in charge who has impeccable taste and unlimited resources. He will devote himself to that task, and all I will have to do is enjoy it when it's done." He looked at his watch. "Can you be ready for dinner at seven-thirty?"

"Probably. Will an LBD do?"

"A Little Black Dress will be fine."

S he reappeared in the living room wearing a quite spectacular LBD and very beautiful jewelry. He escorted her down the hall to the restaurant, which was on the same floor. Shortly they were seated at a table with a view, in the distance, of St. Peter's Basilica. A moon hung over the city, and the drinks were good. They had just finished their first course when Hedy pointed past him. "What's that?" she asked.

He turned and followed her finger. Just past the church a bright light was burning. "Something appears to be on fire," Stone said.

# 5

fter an excellent dinner, Stone signed the bill and stood up. "Do you mind if we take a short walk?" he asked Hedy.

"Not at all."

They took the elevator downstairs and walked past the church, where they found the smoking ruin of the half-built hotel that Stone, with Marcel, had just bought. A single fire truck was spraying water on the smoking ruin, and Marcel was standing alone, disconsolately watching.

Stone approached and introduced Marcel and Hedy. "What happened?" he asked.

"It burned down."

"Do we know why?"

Marcel shook his head. "There's a bright side, though."

"And what would that be?"

"We can rebuild immediately. All we have to do is to occupy the same footprint. The architects will like that, since they won't be stuck with the previous floor plans."

"Whose insurance is going to cover this?"

"The previous owner's. We're not due to close until the day after tomorrow. They should clear the lot, as well. If you'll excuse me, I want to go and speak to the architects in New York. We have the construction company lined up, but I want to see if we can start them with the plans we have." Marcel shook hands and got into his car, and Stone and Hedy started back to the Hassler.

"Why only one fire truck?" she asked.

"I don't know—that would have been a three-alarm fire in New York."

When they were back in the suite, Hedy turned her back. "Will you unzip me, please?"

"It's one of the things I do best," Stone replied, unzipping the dress and kissing her on the shoulder.

"Do I have to sleep in the guest room tonight?"

"You will be most welcome in the master suite."

"I'll be with you shortly."

Stone filled out the breakfast card, hung it on the doorknob, and was already in bed when Hedy slipped in beside him and cuddled close. She was tall and slim, and they fit well together.

"Sorry about your virtue," Stone said, turning toward her.

"That's all right, I can always get it back later," she said.

The following morning they were awakened by the doorbell. Stone got into a robe and let room service wheel the tray into the bedroom. He signed the check and sent the waiter on his way. "May I serve you?" he asked Hedy.

"What a good idea," she said, rearranging the pillows. "What are we having?"

"Eggs Benedict."

"Good choice."

"When is your apartment available?"

"I spoke to the agent. I can get in tomorrow."

"Do you have to?"

"Not necessarily. What did you have in mind?"

"The weather forecast is good. Why don't we rent a car and drive down to Positano, on the Amalfi Coast, for a couple of days? Have you ever been there?"

"No, what's it like?"

"It's better if you experience it, instead of my attempting to describe it. Do you have enough clothes?"

"What will I need?"

"Only a bikini."

She laughed. "I don't think I can dine in a bikini, but I should be able to get by on what I have in my carry-on. What about you?"

"My luggage should be delivered this morning. We can head south after lunch."

"Sounds good."

They made love again after breakfast, then Stone's luggage arrived, and he unpacked, then packed again for Positano.

The phone rang. "Hello?"

"It's Marcel. Good morning."

"And to you, as well. How did you do with the architects?"

"We're in good shape there. They're doing a quick review of the lower floors, and we'll be ready to start in a week. The construction company is on hold."

"I thought I would rent a car and go down to Positano for a couple of days. Can you proceed without me?"

"Of course, and I'll lend you a car—no need to rent. When would you like it?"

"One o'clock?"

"The Hassler doorman will have it for you."

They said goodbye and hung up. Stone called the concierge and asked him to book them into Le Sirenuse, in Positano, then he arranged to cash a check for three thousand euros at the front desk. Stone put a thousand into his pocket and the rest into his briefcase, along with his passport, international driving license and checkbook, laptop, and a spare wristwatch.

At one o'clock they and their luggage were loaded into a Mercedes S550, courtesy of Marcel. The bags went into the trunk, and Stone put his briefcase on the rear floor behind the driver's seat, so that he would have ready access to it. He loaded the address of their Positano hotel into the GPS, and they drove away on schedule.

They left the city and got onto the autostrada, headed south. The weather was sunny and warm, and traffic moved freely.

"Where do you live in New York?" Stone asked.

"I have a loft in SoHo. I live and work there. Do you know the area?"

"Sort of. I get a nosebleed if I go below Forty-second Street, so I don't hang out downtown."

"Where do you live?"

"In Turtle Bay. Do you know it?"

"I once went to see Katharine Hepburn there," she said. "I was supposed to paint her for *Vanity Fair*, but she didn't like my preliminary sketches, and they replaced me with Annie Leibovitz. Ms. Hepburn preferred photographs. Nice neighborhood, though."

"Ms. Hepburn was a neighbor, sort of. I didn't know her, but I saw her come and go sometimes."

They were somewhere east of Naples when Hedy expressed an interest in a pit stop. Stone pulled into an autostrada service area, and they both went inside. He used the men's, then got a cup of coffee and went outside to meet her. As they walked across the parking lot, Stone stopped in his tracks.

"What is it?" she asked.

Stone pointed ahead of them. "Our car is gone."

# 6

aybe he had made a mistake, he thought. He looked over the whole parking lot: there was no black Mercedes S550 parked there.

"Are you sure?" Hedy asked. "Maybe we parked on the other side."

"It was right *there*," he said, pointing.

"Oh, I remember—a truck pulled in next to us as we were getting out of the car."

"There's no truck there, either."

"Uh, Stone, my handbag was in the car."

"What was in it?"

"Everything. Passport, money, iPhone—absolutely *everything*."

"That pretty much covers it for me, too. Plus half my clothes."

"We should call the police," she said.

"Great idea. Do you know how to call the police in Italy?"

"No."

"Neither do I."

"Then we'd better ask somebody for help."

"Another great idea. How's your Italian?"

"Where are we?"

"I have no idea," Stone said. "And I wouldn't know how to tell the police to find us. I don't even know the name of this service area. All I know is, it's somewhere east of Naples."

"Do you have any money? All mine was in my bag, and my credit cards, too."

"I've got a thousand euros in my pocket and my credit cards. Come on." He led her back inside the service stop and went into the shop. He found a map of Italy, took it to the cashier, and bought it. "Do you speak English?" he asked the cashier.

"Little bit."

Stone opened the map. "Where are we?"

She looked at the map and pointed. "Here," she said.

"Thank you."

Stone took his iPhone from its holster.

"Who are you calling?" Hedy asked.

"American Express." He dialed the number on the

back of his credit card and pressed the number on the menu for concierge. He gave them his name and card number.

"How may we help you, Mr. Barrington?"

Stone gave her the name of the service area. "My car has been stolen. I need a car and driver as soon as possible to drive us to Positano."

"I'm so sorry for your trouble," the woman said. "Please hold for a moment."

Stone held.

"You don't want to go back to Rome?" Hedy asked.

"Do you? I think Positano will be more fun. In the circumstances."

"How will we get back to Rome?"

"We'll rent a car."

"But we don't have any clothes."

"There are many shops in Positano and Amalfi."

After about ten minutes, American Express came back on. "Mr. Barrington, I have a car and driver for you. What is your destination in Positano?"

"Le Sirenuse, a hotel."

"The car will be there in approximately forty-five minutes," she said.

"We'll be in the restaurant."

"The car is a Lancia sedan, and the driver's name is Fabrioso. Everything will be charged to your Centurion card."

"Thank you very much." He hung up. "Forty-five minutes. Let's get some lunch."

They got a hot lunch in the cafeteria and sat down. Stone called Joan and told her what had happened. "Call my insurance company," he said, "and make a claim." He dictated a list of his things in the car, then turned to Hedy. "Give me a list of your possessions," he said. "As much as you can remember." She did so.

"They're going to want a police report," Joan said.

"I'll deal with that later," he said. "Thanks for your help, Joan."

"I hope this turns out all right," Joan said, then hung up.

"What time is it in New York?" he asked Hedy.

"Eight AM."

Stone called another number, one he knew well.

"Bacchetti," Dino said.

"It's Stone. Sorry to call you so early."

"Don't worry about it. Where are you?"

"At an autostrada service area east of Naples. My borrowed car has been stolen, along with my briefcase and luggage and my companion's things, as well. I don't know how to call the police in Italy."

"I'll deal with that. Where can they find you?"

"In Positano, at a hotel called Le Sirenuse, in a

couple of hours. A car is on the way to pick us up. I need to file a report with the police for my insurance company."

"I'll take care of it. You okay?"

"I'm fine."

"And the companion?"

"She's fine, too." Stone looked up; a young Italian man in a dark suit was standing there. "Mr. Barrington?"

"Yes."

"I am Fabrioso. Please call me Fabri. Are you ready to go to Positano?"

"We certainly are."

"Where is your luggage?"

"I wish I knew." He explained the situation, then they followed him to the car and got into the rear seat.

"To Le Sirenuse, correct?"

"Correct."

They were on the autostrada for a few minutes, then got off at the exit for Sorrento. Soon they were driving very slowly along a narrow road cut into the mountainside to their left, with a vertical drop to the sea on the other side.

"This is spectacular," Hedy said.

"Sorry about the road. It was built for goat carts, I think."

A giant tour bus appeared from around a bend and nearly nudged them over the side of the cliff.

"Certainly wasn't built for tour buses," Hedy said.

They entered the village of Positano, which clung precariously to the mountainside, then turned down a street toward the sea. Shortly, they pulled into Le Sirenuse.

Stone gave Fabri fifty euros, then went to the front desk and registered.

"Your suite is ready, Mr. Barrington," the desk clerk said, "and there are two gentlemen from the police waiting for you over there." He nodded toward a sofa.

Stone went over and introduced himself to the two men. They spent an hour going over his story and filling out a form and listing everything lost. The desk clerk made a copy for Stone.

Stone thanked the policemen and followed the clerk to their suite, which was spacious, with a large terrace overlooking the village below them and the sea.

"This is absolutely spectacular," Hedy said. "I'm glad you didn't try to explain it to me."

Stone glanced at his watch. "Dinner in an hour?"

"Fine."

His cell phone buzzed. "Hello?"

"It's Dino. Did the cops show?"

"Thanks, they were waiting for us when we arrived at the hotel."

"For what it's worth, they think it's a professional job. Not just anybody can get a Mercedes started without a key."

"That makes sense, I guess."

"Let me know if there's anything else I can do."

"I will. Thanks again." They both hung up.

"It was a professional job," he said to Hedy.

# 7

They woke with sunlight pouring into the suite and had breakfast on the terrace. The day was comfortably warm.

"Shall we do some shopping?" Stone asked. "It's on me. I'll charge the insurance company."

"That's the best offer I've had in years," she said.

Stone went downstairs and inquired about transportation. The most sensible thing available was a small, four-wheeled electric car, much like a motorcycle, with tandem seating.

Hedy got into the backseat, and Stone drove.

"This is a lot better for these roads than a big Mercedes," Hedy said.

"It's more fun, too," Stone replied, accelerating up the hill to the main road. In half an hour they were in Amalfi, which was more a city than a village, and sufficed as an elegant shopping mall. Stone walked into the Ermenegildo Zegna shop and found a lightweight blazer that fit him very well plus a couple of pairs of trousers, some shirts, and a small suitcase. Then he loosed Hedy upon half a dozen shops—Prada, Gucci, Ferragamo, and others.

They packed their things into their new suitcases, strapped them to the top of their vehicle, and drove back to Positano. As they turned off the main road and down the hill toward their hotel, Stone saw flashing blue lights and smoke rising. It took them a good half hour to make their way through the backed-up traffic to Le Sirenuse. In the forecourt of the hotel was the smoking ruin of a car that could barely be recognized as a Mercedes.

"Is that our car?" Hedy asked.

"I think it used to be," Stone said. He took the car key from his pocket and pressed a button. The car beeped, and the lights flashed. "It's ours." He saw the hotel's manager standing nearby and introduced himself. "I believe that's the car that was stolen from us yesterday," he said to the man. "Did anyone see how it got here?"

"A young man drove it into the forecourt, then got out and walked away, according to the doorman," the man replied. "Have you offended someone?" he asked, with a flicker of incredulity.

"Not intentionally," Stone said. "I've only been in Italy for two days."

"You might see if any of your belongings can be recovered, before the firemen haul it away," the man said. "The doorman managed to use a fire extinguisher on it before the firemen arrived." He explained to the firemen that the car belonged to Stone, and he was allowed to approach it.

He removed his briefcase and Hedy's purse from the rear seat: both were charred, but their contents seemed unharmed. Stone used his key to try to open the trunk. It worked. A bellman came and removed their luggage, which seemed unharmed.

Before they could get to their suite, the two policemen he had spoken to the day before were back; they checked things off the list of lost items that had been reported the day before and issued Stone a new police report. "Your insurance will be happy," one of them said.

Upstairs, they unpacked their bags, and Stone transferred the contents of his ruined briefcase to a shopping bag. Realizing that he had neglected to call Marcel duBois the day before, he did so now.

Marcel reacted to the news of the loss of his car with equanimity. "I will notify my insurer," he said.

"I think you should ask for a new car," Stone suggested. "It would cost them less than restoring the present one."

"Quite."

"Marcel, do you think there is a connection between the theft and burning of the car and the burning of the hotel?"

"Possibly," Marcel replied.

"Would you care to expand on that?"

"Not at the present time. When will you return to Rome?"

"Tomorrow, I suppose."

"What time will you depart?"

"After lunch."

"I will send another car for you."

"We can rent one."

"It will be safer if I send a car."

Stone refrained from mentioning that there was evidence to contradict that statement. "All right," he said.

They had lunch on their terrace, and Hedy surprised him by stripping naked and disporting herself on a chaise longue. "I forgot to buy a bikini," she said.

"Who's complaining?" He took off his clothes and joined her.

\*    \*    \*

They awoke later in the afternoon when the sun was behind an awning and a cool breeze swept over them. They took a shower together, made love on the bed, and fell asleep again.

They went down to dinner at the hotel's terrace restaurant. Another couple, apparently Italian, from their conversation, were seated at the next table, quite close to theirs.

Well," Hedy said when they were on coffee, "I must say, Stone, there's never a dull moment being with you."

"I try to keep things interesting," he replied.

"And I've gotten half a new wardrobe out of it, as well. What's next?"

"Only time can tell."

The woman of the couple at the next table, much younger than her companion, got up and headed toward the ladies' room.

"Excuse me," the man said to Stone. He was in his sixties, Stone reckoned, suntanned, well-barbered, and dressed in elegant resort clothing. "I couldn't help noticing your car this afternoon." His English was lightly accented, with overtones of New York.

"It was noticeable, wasn't it?" Stone admitted.

The man offered his hand. "My name is Leonardo Casselli."

"I'm Stone Barrington." He shook the hand and found it soft but strong. "This is Hedy Kiesler. Your name has a familiar ring. Where might I have heard it?"

"Apparently, you read New York's trashier newspapers," Casselli said.

"Ah, Leo Casselli."

"Americans tend toward diminutives," he said. "Please call me Leonardo."

Leo Casselli had been known in New York as a Mafia don for many years, until he either fled to Italy or was deported, Stone didn't remember which. "As you wish," he said.

"I know your name, too," Casselli said.

"I'm surprised," Stone said.

"We had a mutual, ah, acquaintance in the late Eduardo Bianchi."

That did not surprise Stone, since (1) his good friend Eduardo had had a wide circle of acquaintances, and (2) his circle had included some of the Italian-American demimonde. "A lovely man," Stone said.

"He was that," Casselli agreed, "to those he liked and respected. To others, well . . ."

"Like most of us." Stone wondered to which group Casselli had belonged.

The young woman returned to the table, and Casselli rose before she could sit down.

"You must excuse us," Casselli said, "we have another engagement. It was interesting to meet you. And your car."

"Good evening to you," Stone replied.

"Perhaps the car was a warning," Casselli said. "Perhaps you should heed it." Then, without another word, he left.

# 8

Stone and Heddy went back to their suite; Stone called Dino.

"So," Dino said, "is your Italian adventure improving?"

Stone had to think about that for a minute.

"Hello?"

"Sort of," Stone was finally able to say.

"Define 'sort of.'"

"Well, we got most of our stuff back."

"The Italian cops caught the thieves?"

"No, the thieves returned the car, with our stuff still inside it."

"Well, that's a win-win, isn't it?"

"Not exactly."

"Why not?"

"The car was a total loss—the thieves set it on fire. In front of our hotel."

"Did you report that to the police?"

"We didn't have to, they turned up almost immediately. Their big action was to revise the police report to exclude the items returned."

"Okay," Dino said. "That makes sense. Anything else?"

"Nothing. They ventured no information on the thieves or their motive."

"I see," Dino said, clearly not seeing.

"Something else, though: at dinner I found myself sitting next to Leo Casselli."

"Casselli? He got deported, didn't he?"

"Deported to Italy. He may have self-deported, I don't remember."

"And how did you come to be seated next to him?"

"Luck of the draw, I guess. He was there with a very young lady."

"And did you and Casselli converse?"

"We did. He pointed out that we had a mutual acquaintance in Eduardo Bianchi."

"I'm not entirely surprised that he knew Eduardo. I'll bet they hadn't spoken for forty years."

"I didn't ask, but if I see him again, I will."

"What makes you think you'll see him again?"

"He expressed an interest in my burned-out car—or rather, in Marcel duBois's burned-out car. He said that maybe it was a warning, and that maybe I should heed it."

"Uh-oh."

"Funny, that's what I said to myself."

"Are you mixed up in something Casselli is interested in?"

"I don't know, but I'm here for a board meeting, which was about buying a partially built hotel that we could turn into a new Arrington. That was at midday yesterday. Then yesterday evening the structure burned down."

"Uh-oh."

"You said that before."

"Sounds like you and Casselli have a common interest."

"Not in the sense that we are partners."

"Casselli may not see it that way."

"I thought he was retired."

"He's retired from America, although he may still have hidden assets here, but he could still be active in Italy. I'll check into that."

"Good idea."

"When are you going back to Rome?"

"Marcel is sending a car for us tomorrow afternoon. We should be back later in the day."

"Let me talk to a couple of people, and I'll get back to you late tomorrow."

"Okay."

"And in the meantime, try not to piss off any mafiosi, will you?"

"I haven't *been* trying." They hung up.

W hat was that all about?" Hedy asked.

"I'm not sure. Dino is going to make some calls and get back to me tomorrow."

"Tell me who Dino is, if you haven't already."

"He's the police commissioner of New York City."

"And you know him how?"

"I used to be a cop, and Dino and I were partners."

"And you keep in touch?"

"We're sort of best friends."

"That must be very convenient for you."

"Sometimes."

"Is Dino how we got our stuff back?"

"I don't think so. Apparently, there's something going on that I didn't know about. I'm going to have to have a serious talk with my partner, Marcel, when we get back to Rome."

# 9

The following morning they took the little electric vehicle and roamed the vertically stacked streets of Positano, doing a little light shopping for Hedy. They checked out of Le Sirenuse at one o'clock, and there was a Mercedes with a driver waiting for them. Stone got a better look at the Amalfi Coast with somebody else driving, and he enjoyed the experience, until they got onto the autostrada, when the driver spoke up.

"Mr. Barrington," he said, "is there any reason somebody would be following you?"

"None that I'm aware of."

"There's a black Lancia sedan three cars back," the man said. "It's been behind us since we left your hotel."

Stone looked back and saw the car; two men occupied the front seat.

"How fast are we going?"

"A hundred and thirty kilometers an hour."

"Let's see what happens at a hundred and sixty."

The Mercedes accelerated. "He's keeping pace with us," the driver said.

"What's going on?" Hedy asked.

"Somebody appears to be tailing us."

"Are we in any danger?"

"I don't think so, they're keeping well back."

"I hope you're right."

"So do I." Stone put his head back and dozed off.

When he woke up they were in Rome. "Do you want to go to your apartment or come with me?" he asked Hedy.

"I spoke to the rental agent while you were asleep, and I asked the driver to drop me there. Let me get sorted out, and I'll come to you later."

"I'd like that—you're good company."

"So are you."

The driver dropped Hedy under an arch in a narrow street and took her bags to the elevator.

"I'd like to go to Mr. duBois's office," Stone said. Ten minutes later, they were driving under a larger arch and into a spacious courtyard. "Can you take my luggage to the Hassler, please?"

"Of course, sir. Should I come back for you?"

"I'll get a cab," Stone said. "Whatever happened to the Lancia following us?"

"He kept with us all the way."

Stone got out and went into the building, where a uniformed security guard called duBois, then he was sent to the top floor.

Marcel greeted him at the elevator. "Come in, Stone," he said, and ushered him to a comfortable sitting room.

"This is a lot like your Paris home," Stone said, looking around.

"When you live in several places, it's best to keep them as much alike as possible. That way, I always know where everything is."

Marcel served Stone an espresso, then sat down.

"What's going on, Marcel? I was followed here from Positano by two men in a car. Were they your security people?"

"No," Marcel said. "It appears that someone is taking a deep interest in our plans for the new hotel. Perhaps it's related to that."

"Marcel, have you been approached by anyone demanding a bribe?"

"A bribe for what?"

"For anything at all. I'm beginning to feel that the Italian Mafia has taken an interest in our project."

"No one has asked me for money, except the people I've hired for various things. Apart from the fire, everything has been normal."

"Marcel, it is not normal for your car to be stolen at an autostrada service area, then returned to me in Positano and set afire."

Marcel shrugged. "I will grant you that."

"Who is providing security for the hotel site?"

"The same security company that provides people for this building."

"An Italian company?"

"Yes. They were recommended by a business acquaintance."

"Perhaps it would be better if we delayed the acquisition of the hotel site until we've had time to look into this situation."

"Stone, I closed on the site this morning, on schedule. You and I now own it, through the corporation."

"Has anyone made an offer to buy the site from you?"

"No, why would anyone do that?"

"Perhaps someone is trying to frighten you and drive the price down, so they can buy it cheaply."

"Nothing like that has happened," Marcel said. "Everything is normal."

"I'm afraid not," Stone said. "Last night at dinner I found myself seated next to a man called Leo Casselli. Does that name ring a bell?"

"I met someone called Leonardo Casselli at a social function in Paris a couple of weeks ago."

"Same fellow. In New York he was known as Leo, and he was the reputed head of a large Mafia organization. He returned to his native Italy some years ago."

"I've heard nothing from or about him since our meeting," Marcel said.

"I doubt very much if Casselli has retired. My friend Dino Bacchetti is looking into it. Casselli introduced himself to me, and as he left the table he said that maybe the burning of the car was a warning, and that perhaps I should heed it."

"That sounds ominous," Marcel said.

"I thought so, too."

"What do you propose we do?" Marcel asked.

"I think we have to wait and see if Casselli approaches us, then, if he does, make a decision."

"All right," Marcel replied. As he spoke, a telephone beside him buzzed, and he picked it up. "Yes?" Marcel listened, then covered the phone. "Mr. Casselli is on the line," he said.

"Don't speak to him just yet," Stone said.

"Please tell the gentleman that I'm in a meeting

and can't be disturbed," Marcel said, then hung up the phone. "Now what, Stone?"

"I think we have to make some preparations before speaking to Casselli," he said. "I think that we should start by replacing all your security people with guards from Strategic Services, Mike Freeman's company."

"I have a contract with the Italian company," Marcel said.

"Then I had better read the contract."

Marcel picked up the phone and ordered the contract brought to him.

Stone went through it. "The contract is up for renewal in three weeks," he said. "I suggest you get Mike's people in, then buy out the remaining time on that contract."

"Call Mike," Marcel said.

# *IO*

tone called Mike Freeman in New York.

"Where are you?" Mike asked.

"In Rome. May I assume you have an office here?"

"You may."

"I'm here with Marcel duBois," Stone said. "I expect you remember taking over his security needs in Paris last year."

"Of course."

"He has something like the same situation now in Rome. We're trying to build a new Arrington here, and I'm beginning to suspect that the local Mafia is taking an interest. You remember Leo Casselli?"

"I remember reading about him."

"He's back in Italy." Stone told him about his encounter with Casselli and about the two fires.

"How quickly do you want my people there?"

"As quickly as possible, and I'd like you to be particularly careful that none of your people has any Mafia connections."

"How many do you need?"

"The current contract with an Italian company calls for twelve."

"I've got four Americans there who speak good Italian. Let's start with them and then go to Italians who speak English."

"Sounds good."

"I can have at least half a dozen on-site tomorrow morning and the rest soon after. I'll send in some people from Paris, if necessary."

"Excellent." Stone gave him the address. "Have your supervisor come to Marcel's apartment on the top floor of the building, then he can start moving his people in."

"All right. Are you staying there?"

"I'm at the Hassler, but the best way to reach me is on my cell. And we're going to need the new hotel building site guarded, too."

"We'll assess that tomorrow morning and make a recommendation, and that will include a sweep of the offices for devices and a thorough examination of Marcel's computer systems."

"Good."

"I'd better get started, then, we're near the end of the business day in Rome."

"Thanks, Mike." Stone hung up. "Mike can make the transition tomorrow morning. His supervisor will come here and speak to you, then he'll move his people in. It should go smoothly."

"Wonderful," Marcel said. "I'm much relieved."

"We don't want a repeat of our encounter with the Russians in Paris," Stone said. "It's best to draw a clear line now."

"I agree."

Marcel's phone rang again, and a conversation ensued. He hung up. "That was our construction company," he said. "They're withdrawing from the project, and they wouldn't give me a clear explanation of why."

"I think we know why," Stone said. "You should speak to the architects in New York and see who they can recommend to take over the project. Explain to them what we're facing here."

"Of course."

"If you'll excuse me, I'll go back to the Hassler and make some calls of my own."

"Good. We'll talk tomorrow."

Stone took the elevator downstairs and walked through the courtyard to the street, where he found a cab almost immediately. Back at the Hassler, he called Joan.

"How is sunny Rome?"

"Sunny. I need you to order me a new briefcase from the guy who made the one I have. I'd like it identical, but an inch deeper."

"All right. I don't know how long that will take."

"Let's get him started."

"Something happen to the old one?"

"It was damaged in a fire. I'll explain when I see you."

"And when will that be?"

"I don't know yet. Probably another few days, maybe a week."

"Having too much fun to come home?"

"I'll tell you all when I get back."

"Okay, I'm on the briefcase." They hung up.

His phone rang. "Hello?"

"It's Hedy. I'm all sorted out here. Are you ready for me?"

"Come ahead," he said. "I'm more than ready."

"I'll be there in less than an hour."

"I'll look forward to seeing you."

"Yes, it's been such a long time, hasn't it?"

They hung up, and Stone stretched out on the bed for a nap. He was nearly asleep when he was wakened by the doorbell. He had forgotten to put out the DO NOT DISTURB sign. He got out of bed and answered it.

A bellman stood at the door, holding an elongated cardboard box. "Flowers for you, Mr. Barrington," the man said.

Stone put out the DO NOT DISTURB sign and opened the box. Who would be sending him flowers? Hardly anyone knew he was in Rome.

The box was filled with lilies, and they were wilted and dying. Stone found a card and read it.

*You would be more comfortable in New York.*

Stone called Mike with the latest.

"I'm going to put somebody on you," Mike said. "This is going to escalate, and we have to be ready."

"Whatever you think is best."

"I'll have somebody with you in the morning."

# II

Hedy arrived at the Hassler and let herself into the suite. Stone was back on the bed, and she lay down with him and put her head on his shoulder. "I hope this all goes away soon," she said.

"I don't think that's going to happen," Stone said, "and I can't just go back to New York and leave Marcel to handle it. We had a similar problem with the Russian Mob in Paris. Marcel is known there as the French Warren Buffett, and he was and is accustomed to a certain deference in the way people deal with him. I don't think it's something he's sought, it's just happened as his reputation has grown. I believe the experience with the Russians, though, has toughened him up. He's already expressed a willingness to do what's necessary to deal with the problem."

"How can I help?" Hedy asked.

"First of all, consider your own position: these people already know about you from Positano, and your association with me could cause you difficulties. I'm happy to pay off the agent for the apartment and send you back to New York, or wherever you want to go, on the next airplane."

"You'd be happy to see me go?"

"Don't misunderstand—I'm conflicted. I want you with me, but I don't want you to be less than safe and comfortable."

"I feel both safe and comfortable with you," she said.

"I'm glad of that, but if at any time you want to distance yourself from the situation, I'll get you out."

"I'll keep that in mind."

Stone had a thought. "Excuse me," he said, "I have to call Pat Frank in New York." He moved the pillows around and sat up in bed.

"Who's he?"

"It's a she. She runs an aircraft management business, and I'm her client." He dialed the number.

"Pat Frank."

"Hi, it's Stone."

"You okay?"

"Yes, but I had to make an unexpected trip to Rome a couple of days ago, and I'd like you to find a ferry pilot and move my airplane over here. Is there a convenient general aviation airport here?"

"Yes, there's Ciampino, southeast of the city, just outside Rome's autostrada beltway. How long do you need hangar space?"

"I'm not sure: a week or ten days, maybe."

"I have a pilot in mind: I'll give him a call, then check on hangar space and get back to you."

"Okay. Use the cell number. And don't use my name on any of the paperwork." He hung up.

"You really do have an airplane?" Hedy asked. "I thought you were kidding."

"I really do, and I fly it myself."

"I feel like a drink," she said, getting up. "Can I get you one?"

"Sure."

She came back shortly with two glasses, then Stone's phone rang.

"Hello?"

"It's Pat. I've got you a pilot, and he can leave early tomorrow morning. From Teterboro, right?"

"Right."

"I'll flight-plan him to the Azores, he'll overnight there, then on to Lisbon and Rome. The airplane will be there the day after tomorrow, and the name for the hangar reservation is under Pat Frank, Inc. The FBO is Sky Services." She gave him the address, phone number, and a contact name. "When you're ready to fly out, call me and I'll take care of the flight planning and a hotel in the Azores."

"Good. Have the pilot check the fluids and top off the tanks as soon as he arrives in Rome, and you can send Joan a bill for his services, expenses, and the fuel."

"Will do. Have a good time in Rome."

"I'll do my best." He hung up and took a sip of his drink. "There, now we'll have a quick way out of town, if we need it."

She laughed. "I don't think I've ever needed a quick way out of town before."

"That's what happens when you hang out with disreputable characters."

"Or just someone who leads an interesting life."

"I warn you, sometimes it gets a little too interesting."

"I'm on board. Shall we order in some dinner?"

"You call room service."

"What would you like?"

"Surprise me. I feel like a shower." He knocked off the remainder of his drink, stripped off his clothes, and stood under a stream of hot water for ten minutes.

\*　　\*　　\*

Room service arrived, and Stone approved of Hedy's choices. They were on coffee when Stone's phone rang.

"Hello?"

"It's Mike. I've made some calls in Rome, and I don't like what I'm hearing. I want to get you out of your hotel and into an apartment. I've got someone making calls about that now."

"Hang on, Mike." He turned to Hedy. "My friend Mike Freeman, who's handling our security, wants us out of the hotel."

"How about my apartment?"

"Does anyone besides you and me know about it?"

"A couple of people in New York." She gave him the address.

Stone went back to Mike. "I've got an apartment in the Via Stelletto, Pantheon district."

"All right, get packed. I'll have somebody there in half an hour to get you out. Don't check out of the hotel—I'll deal with that."

"All right," Stone said. He hung up. "Let's get packed."

Half an hour later there was a soft knock at the door.

"Who is it?" Stone asked.

"I'm from Mike Freeman."

Stone opened the door to find a large man in a dark suit; he had a hotel trolley with him. They gave him their luggage and followed him to a service elevator, then out a service exit to a waiting van with a driver. Stone gave them the address.

"I know it," the driver said. "It has a courtyard, which is good for us."

"There were two men in a car out front at the hotel," the big man said. "I think they were waiting for you. Don't worry, we'll lose them."

They followed what seemed to Stone a torturous route. As they turned into the Via Stelletto, the big man got out of the van, while the driver continued into the street and turned into the courtyard. "He's just making sure nobody's on our tail," the driver said. The big man rejoined them, and they got their luggage and the two of them into a tiny elevator, while the big man ran up the four flights of stairs.

He didn't seem winded when they arrived. "Do you mind if I have a look around before you go in?" he asked.

"Help yourself," Hedy said, unlocking the door.

He disappeared inside, then returned a couple of minutes later. "It's good," he said, and he took their bags inside. "Nobody can see into the place, and the terrace overlooks the courtyard, not the street. I couldn't have picked a better place myself."

Stone had a look around: there was a large kitchen, two bedrooms and baths, and a comfortable living room, plus a large terrace accessed through French doors. "Very nice," he said.

"My name's Hal," the big man said. He handed Stone two cell phones. "One for each of you. Use them for outgoing calls. You can use your own phone for incoming ones. I'll be in or around the courtyard downstairs tonight. A guy named Ernie will relieve me in the morning, and he'll check in with you. My phone number is speed dial one, his is two, three will get you Mr. Freeman, in New York." He took Stone aside and handed him a compact 9mm handgun and a spare magazine. "It's loaded, and there's one in the chamber," he said.

"Thank you for your help."

"It's what we do. Good night."

He left and Stone went into the bedroom, where Hedy was unpacking his things and putting them into a huge wardrobe on one side of the room. He put the gun in the bedside table drawer.

"Now," she said, finishing her work and handing him a terrycloth robe. "You're my guest."

# *12*

Stone woke to an unfamiliar sound: there was a light knocking far away, and it began to increase in volume. He got into his robe, took the gun from the bedside table drawer, and walked through the living room and the kitchen to the front door. "Who is it?" he shouted, before opening the door.

"Ernie."

Stone unlatched the door and found a smaller version of Hal there.

"Mike Freeman sent me. I just wanted you to know I'm on the job," he said.

Hedy appeared from behind Stone, pulling on a sweater over jeans. "I've got to go out for breakfast stuff," she said.

"Walk her to the store and back, will you?" Stone asked Ernie.

"Sure thing. You gonna be okay?"

Stone nodded.

"Hey," Ernie said, pointing to the edge of the front door. "Give me your door key."

Hedy handed it to him. He inserted and turned it. Six bolts emerged from the door. "Look at that," he said. "It's like a safe: heavy steel and six bolts that go into a steel jamb. Nobody's coming in here without a bazooka."

"Good to know," Stone said. He had never seen a door like that, either.

Hedy let herself out.

"Lock it from outside," Stone said, and she did.

Stone got a shower and a shave, and by the time he was out of the bathroom, Hedy had come back and had scrambled eggs and Italian sausage ready.

"Really good," Stone said. "You know, there's something very familiar about your name, and I can't place it."

"Hedy Eva Maria Kiesler? It's the real name of the actress from the forties, Hedy Lamarr. She's Viennese, as was my father, and he claimed some sort of kinship, a distant cousin or something. The name is a family joke."

"'I am Tondelayo,'" Stone quoted. "That was her famous line from *White Cargo*. She was very beautiful."

"Very smart, too. She invented some sort of torpedo that was used in World War Two. She had several patents, I think."

"So you skipped the mechanical talent and went straight for the artistic?"

"Something like that. I can pick a lock, though, if it's not too complicated."

"Good—you never know when you'll need a lock picked."

"I want to start to work today," she said. "Will that disturb you?"

"No more than you usually disturb me. There are a lot of books in the living room. I'll see if I can find something in English."

After breakfast, Hedy set up her easel on the terrace, and Stone found a collection of Mark Twain pieces. They were both fully occupied until noon, then they went out to look for some lunch, with Ernie a dozen paces back, watching everything like a predatory bird.

They found a workingman's tiny café a few doors up the street and had some lasagna, then took a stroll around the neighborhood. There were a couple of dozen restaurants within a five-minute walk, and the Pantheon, the ancient pagan Roman temple that featured the world's largest unsupported dome, a ten-minute walk away. They continued to the Piazza Navona, with its three Bernini fountains and a zillion tourists.

They were back at the apartment by three, and Stone's phone was ringing.

"Hello?"

"It's Mike. Everything okay?"

"Yes. Your guys got us out and to the apartment safely, and Hal approves of our security here."

"My people made the transition at Marcel's offices and apartment on schedule this morning. The Italian guards are out, and I've got more people arriving about now from our Paris office."

"You said last night that you were hearing things. What things?"

"My people are hearing that the local Mob have taken a very big interest in Marcel and you. They apparently see the new hotel as a gold mine for them in bribes and extortion. My tech guy went through the security system and computers at Marcel's office and found the phones bugged, and the computer network breached. All that has been taken care of, and new defenses have been installed."

"Do you think you can get a message to Leo Casselli?"

"Probably. What do you want me to tell him?"

"Just let him know that we're not going to play his game, that he'd be smart to leave us alone."

"I think the disconnection of his electronic surveillance will tell him that. In the meantime, you need to be on guard for some sort of more physical approach. Beware of getting yanked into a car, and don't either of you go out without Ernie or Hal."

"Are we doing enough? Anything we're missing?"

"I've spoken to Dino, who's spoken to somebody in the Rome police, and I think that's all we can do, until they make another move."

"Okay, I'll keep you posted on what's going on at this end."

"Same from here." They hung up, and Stone went back to his Mark Twain.

As darkness was falling that evening, and they were contemplating dinner at a restaurant, Stone's second phone rang.

"It's Ernie," he said. "Lock that fucking bank vault door of yours." He hung up.

# *13*

tone locked the door.

"What's up?" Hedy asked.

"I don't know, Ernie said to lock the door."

"Would you like a drink?" she asked.

"Not right now. I want to find out what's happening, first." There was a sharp metallic rapping on the door, and Stone walked over to it. "Who is it?"

"Hal."

Stone unlocked the door, and Hal walked in.

"We made a couple of bad guys in the neighborhood and watched them for a few minutes. They appeared to be searching, and they finally got into a car and left."

"That's good. Do you think they know we're in the neighborhood?"

"Possibly."

"How could they?"

"Have you used your own phone today?"

"No, I used the one you gave me."

"Let me see your iPhone."

Stone handed it over.

Hal removed the SIM card and handed it to Stone. "Don't put this into the phone until you want to use it." He did the same to Hedy's iPhone. "It could be that they picked up on one or both of your phones when you were at the Hassler and tracked them to this street but weren't able to localize on the apartment. This is a densely populated neighborhood, and even with a signal they might be unable to zero in on you. For instance, even if they got the building right, they wouldn't be able to tell what floor you're on. The good news is, we were able to put a tracker on their car, so if it returns, we'll get a heads-up on our receiving equipment."

"That's good to know."

"What are your dinner plans?"

"We haven't made any."

"I don't want you to get cabin fever. There's a nice place directly across the street from you, with a name something like Italian for white cat. Try that."

"Okay."

"Somebody will have eyes on you all the time, and if we spot anybody, we'll handle it. We'll call you if any action on your part is needed. Don't carry the gun—somebody might spot it, and we don't want to cause a fuss."

"As you wish."

"I'd go to dinner no later than seven," Hal said. "That will guarantee you a table, and the place will be crowded later."

Hal let himself out of the apartment, and Stone locked the door behind him.

"How about that drink now?" Hedy asked.

"What are my choices?"

"Is Knob Creek okay?"

"Where on earth did you get that?"

"I found it in a shop down the street, amazingly enough. They had two bottles, and I bought both of them." She poured them each a drink.

"I didn't know you were a bourbon drinker," he said.

"I'm a Georgia girl, little town called Delano. We didn't even have a liquor store, but we managed."

"How did Arthur Steele become your stepfather?"

"My mother moved to New York when I was in college, and she got a job at an insurance agency. She met Arthur there, when he came to see her boss. Next thing I knew, she was married to him and living on Fifth Avenue. They invited me up for Thanksgiving, and that was the first time I met him."

"Was it love at first sight for the two of you?"

"No, but we got along. He was nice enough to give me a trust fund, the income from which has allowed me to be a painter. It took me ten years to start making a living from selling my work."

"Arthur must have a soft spot for you."

"He has a soft spot for my mother, and whatever it cost him, it was worth it not to have her worrying about whether I was starving. Arthur is a pragmatic man."

At seven they walked across the street to the little restaurant, and it turned out to be very good.

"I guess I'm going to have to get used to having Italian food every night," Hedy said.

"That's no strain for me," Stone said. "I love Italian food." There were no spirits available, so he ordered a bottle of Amarone.

Stone's phone rang. "Hello?"

"It's Hal. The car we bugged is back in the neighborhood. Be prepared to leave cash on the table and leave, if necessary."

"Okay." Stone saw Ernie walk past a window near their table, and he shifted his chair to the other side, so as to face the street.

"Anything wrong?" Hedy asked.

"Not yet," Stone said.

# 14

Ernie appeared in the restaurant window again. He was looking up the street and held up a hand as if to say, "Stop."

Then he turned, looked directly at Stone, and beckoned.

Stone left cash on the table, took Hedy's hand, and towed her to the door. Ernie walked up. "Just one second," he said, looking up the street again. "When I say go, walk quickly across the street and under the arch."

Stone waited patiently.

"What's happening?" Hedy asked.

"I'll tell you in a minute."

"Go," Ernie said.

Stone took Hedy's hand and hurried her across the street and into the courtyard. When they were on the elevator, Hedy demanded information again.

"Ernie and Hal saw someone who made them uncomfortable," Stone said. "They wanted us to cross the street without being seen."

"Okay," Hedy said. "Is this how we have to live our lives for the next three weeks?"

"You don't have to. If you don't want to go back to New York, I think it's best if I move to a hotel for the duration, whatever that is. Or, if you like, we can go to Paris until things cool off here."

"Why Paris?"

"Because I have a house there."

"God, how many houses do you have?"

"It's a weakness of mine—I like having houses in places I like."

"But not Rome?"

"I haven't spent much time here for a long time. In fact, until this trip, I had never spent much more than a long weekend here."

He let them into the apartment and locked the door behind them.

"I thought you were just an attorney," Hedy said, "but attorneys don't make enough money to have houses all over the place."

"Some attorneys do. I'm also an investor in two privately owned corporations that make money."

"Is one of them the hotel business?"

"Yes."

"What's the other?"

"Strategic Services, who are providing our security."

"All right, tell me where I would be safe."

Stone thought about that. "Hawaii."

"Why Hawaii?"

"It's a long way from here, and it doesn't have a Mafia that I'm aware of."

"Am I safer in Hawaii than in Paris?"

"Paris is just as safe."

"All right, let's go to Paris—at least I can paint there."

There was a rap on the Great Iron Door.

"Who is it?"

"Hal."

Stone opened the door. "We're going to need a ride to Ciampino Airport tomorrow morning, early, before the Mafia wakes up."

"Okay," Hal said. "I'll have a car here. What time?"

"Eight o'clock should be okay."

"Done. Everything okay here?"

"Yes."

"I'll have a look around."

"Go ahead."

Hal disappeared into the apartment; after a moment he came back and crooked a finger at Stone.

Stone followed him into the bedroom. The words *Go Home!* were written on the bedspread in what looked a lot like blood.

Stone whipped the bedspread off the bed, so that Hedy wouldn't see it. "Make it seven AM for the car," he said.

W hile they were having a very early breakfast the following morning, Stone called Pat Frank's office in New York.

"I'd like the airplane out of the hangar, full tanks, file for Le Bourget at eight AM," he said to the person on duty.

"Roger wilco," the young woman said. "Your flight plan will be waiting for you at Sky Services. Do you require catering?"

"No, thanks. Just ask them to be sure the airplane has been topped off with fuel. They were supposed to do it on arrival, but be sure."

"Certainly. We recommend Landmark Aviation at Le Bourget. Would you like hangarage there?"

"Yes, and fueling on arrival."

"And a car and driver into Paris?"

"Yes, please."

"Please let us know if we can be of further help."

"I'll do that." Stone hung up and turned to Hedy. "If you like, you can leave your painting equipment here, and I'll buy you replacements in Paris."

"Good idea. I won't have to pack everything."

They beat the rush hour traffic out of Rome and were at the airport in half an hour. Stone's Citation CJ3+ awaited on the ramp. Hal loaded their luggage while Stone did the preflight inspection.

"You have a choice of seating," Stone said to Hedy. "In the copilot's seat or in the cabin."

"You weren't kidding when you said you flew yourself?"

"Nope."

"I'll take the copilot's seat," she said.

"Do you want me to have you met at the other end?" Hal asked.

"I don't think so, we're not quite so hot in Paris."

He got Hedy seated and buckled in, then closed the door and began running through his checklist. He started the engines, then entered the flight plan into the computer and checked the weather report. Shortly they were at the end of the runway and cleared for takeoff.

"Here we go," Stone said to Hedy.

"What should I hold on to?"

"It's just like the airlines, relax." He pushed the throttles forward and the airplane accelerated quickly. He rotated, then raised the landing gear and the flaps and switched on the autopilot.

Hedy made a swooshing sound.

"Have you been holding your breath?" Stone asked.

"Yes, I didn't even realize it."

"The autopilot is flying the airplane now," he said. "It will continue to do so until we're on final approach to Le Bourget."

"Is that supposed to make me feel better?"

"I don't think anything will make you feel better," Stone said, "but it's too late to get out and walk."

An hour and a half later the airplane touched down at Le Bourget.

"Well, that was fairly painless," Hedy said, when Stone had shut down the engines.

"It usually is," Stone said. Stone got out of the pilot's seat and opened the door. A large car pulled up to the airplane, and Stone unlocked the luggage compartment and began handing the driver their bags.

Reflexively, Stone looked around the ramp for suspicious cars or people. He saw nothing, but somehow, he didn't feel relieved.

# 15

When they arrived at the entrance to Stone's mews in Saint-Germain-des-Prés, the gates were open; Joan had arranged for them to be expected. As they got out of the car, the gates closed.

"Wow," Hedy said, looking around the mews. "This is beautiful."

"That's what I thought when I first saw it," Stone said.

"This is the first thing I'm going to paint," she said.

"And I will be the customer for your painting."

The driver took their bags inside. Stone introduced Hedy to the housekeeper, Marie, who then took the driver and the luggage upstairs to the master suite.

Hedy walked into the living room and looked around. "This is like a beautiful set in a French movie."

"That's not exactly an accident," Stone said. "Although the house was sparsely furnished when I bought it, I hired a woman who has a shop around the corner to decorate it to my specifications. Her shop specializes in supplying movie set designers with furnishings. By the way, there's an artist's supply shop a couple of doors down from her. They should have what you need."

"Then I'm going there now," Hedy said. "Which way?"

"Out the gate, take a right, and it's half a dozen shops down the street." He took a key from a kitchen drawer and gave it to her. "This will get you back in through the door in the gate."

Hedy departed, and Marie returned with the driver. Stone tipped him and sent him on his way.

"Welcome home, Mr. Barrington," Marie said in her heavily accented English. "How long will you be with us?"

"I'm not sure, Marie, a few days, at least."

"I've prepared some food for dinner tonight. May I get you some lunch? Perhaps an omelet?"

"Let's wait until Hedy comes back."

"As you wish." Marie disappeared into the kitchen.

Stone sat down in the living room and phoned Marcel in Rome.

"Hello, Stone, I tried to call you at the Hassler, but you had gone, and your cell phone didn't answer."

"I'm sorry about that, Marcel. The security people insisted that I disable it. I'll have it working again in a few minutes."

"Where are you?"

"In Paris. We had a threat, and I thought it best to get out of town for a bit. How is it going there?"

"Michael Freeman's people have been excellent. It seems that I was not as secure here as I had thought."

"Have there been any incidents since I saw you?"

"Only that Mr. Casselli continues to call each day, and I continue to refuse to speak to him. The new construction company begins today clearing away the ruins of the old hotel. They will be ready to start construction in a week or so. The architects have produced elevations and infrastructure plans already, and they are beautiful. My instructions to them were to make the building look as if it has always been there."

"Perfect."

"I believe Dino has been trying to reach you. He called here a couple of times."

"I'll call him right away."

"Have a good time in Paris. Will you be coming here afterwards?"

"If you need me."

"I'll try not to, but you never know."

Stone said goodbye and then called Dino, who was still in his office.

"Where the hell have you been?"

"I had to disappear for a few days, and Mike's people insisted I disable my cell phone. Not soon enough, though. Casselli's people managed to track me down. We arrived in Paris an hour and a half ago."

"Ah, Paris."

"Why don't you and Viv join me for a few days?"

"I'll see if I can think of a good enough excuse. In the meantime, I've spoken with a man named Massimo Bertelli, in Rome, who is head of the Italian Anti-Mafia Investigative Department, or DIA, and asked him advice on how you should proceed."

"I'd be grateful for his advice," Stone replied.

"He's assigned a special team to monitor your situation and to take such action as is required. He says to stonewall Casselli, to give him nothing. He's unaccustomed to that sort of stand, and it will rattle him."

"That is exactly what Marcel and I have done and will continue to do, though I have to say he's managed to rattle us."

"You're better off in Paris. There's nothing you can do in Rome but advise Marcel, and you can do that on the phone."

"I don't want to run out on Marcel."

"Don't overestimate your importance."

"Gee, thanks."

"Let me talk to Viv and see what her schedule is, then I'll get back to you about coming to Paris."

"Do that, it would be good to see you both." Stone hung up.

Hedy was just coming through the door. "I got what I needed," she said. "Everything will be delivered in an hour."

"Lunch?"

"Great."

"An omelet?"

"Perfect."

Stone went to the kitchen and gave Marie their order.

He went back to the living room, found his cell phone, and reinstalled the SIM chip, then put it into his pocket. Less than a minute passed before it rang. He checked the caller ID window, but got nothing. "Hello?"

"This is Leonardo Casselli," a voice said.

Stone hung up. He removed the SIM chip, then used the landline to call Joan in New York.

"You got there okay?"

"I did. I'd like you to do something for me."

"Okay."

"Please go to the Apple store and buy me a new iPhone, with a new number. Get it authorized and working, then FedEx it to me in Paris."

"You lose the old one?"

"No, I just don't want to use it. I'll back up the new one to the iCloud and get all my files and apps onto the new phone."

"Will do."

Stone put his phone and the SIM chip into his briefcase; he could live a day without using it.

The omelet was perfect.

# 16

After lunch, Hedy took her easel and paints into the mews, picked a spot, set up, and began to paint. Stone found a half-finished book next to his easy chair and set about finishing it. He read until the shadows outside were long, then he put his head back and dozed for a while.

He was awakened by the slamming of the front door. Hedy came into the room, wiping paint from her hands, and kissed him on the forehead. "Sorry about the noise, the door got away from me." She held up the painting.

"Wonderful!" he said. "And sold!"

"It's my gift to you for keeping me entertained and safe, not necessarily in that order."

The phone rang, and Stone picked it up. "Hello?"

"It's Dino. We're booked on a late plane, and we should be at your house by ten tomorrow morning."

"Then I'll put sheets on the bed. See you then." He hung up. "My friend Dino Bacchetti and his wife, Viv, are joining us for a few days. They'll be here mid-morning tomorrow."

"Oh, good. He's the cop, right?"

"New York City's top cop."

"Then I'll feel even safer. When's dinner?"

"At seven."

"Then I'm going to have a bath and change." She kissed him again and went upstairs.

Stone went into the kitchen and asked Marie to get a guest room ready. She nodded, then went on cooking.

T he following morning Stone was awakened by the doorbell, and a moment later Marie knocked on the door and entered. "Federal Express," she said, handing him a package.

"It's my new phone," he said to Hedy, who was stirring.

"Why a new phone?"

"Because Casselli doesn't have the number."

They had breakfast in bed, then showered and

went downstairs to greet their guests. At the stroke of ten, the gate bell rang, and Stone buzzed in the car carrying the Bacchettis. He embraced them both, then introduced them to Hedy, while the driver and Marie made their luggage disappear.

"Breakfast?" he asked them.

"We had it on the plane," Dino said. "Just coffee, after we've cleaned up a little."

They came down looking brighter, and Stone gave them his new phone number. "Put that in your phone," he said to both of them.

"Why the new number?"

"Because Casselli has the old one, and I got tired of hanging up on him."

They settled into the living room for coffee.

"I've done a little research on Casselli," Dino said. "He has a record in New York going back to his teens, but about fifteen years ago he came over all respectable and started giving money to hospitals and museums."

"Sounds like he was using Eduardo Bianchi as his model."

"Maybe so. But he got his fingers caught in a wringer when one of his people started talking to the

FBI. They put the guy in the Witness Protection Program and the U.S. attorney started putting together a RICO indictment for Casselli. He didn't stick around for the service of the papers. He got on a plane to Rome, and he's been there ever since. He has a house in Naples, too, and a place in Positano, where you met him."

"How did the Italian Mob receive him?"

"Coldly, at first, but they warmed up after a couple of big dons suddenly disappeared, never to be heard from again, and pretty soon Casselli was in the driver's seat. It took him a little less than a year. Since then, nobody has challenged him. Except Marcel, of course, and you."

"It's not like we want to take turf from him."

"No, you're already *on* his turf, and he expects to get his pound of flesh from anybody who treads there."

"I don't think I can spare a pound of flesh," Stone said.

"That's my boy, just keep annoying him until he rears up and disappears *you*."

"That's encouraging."

"I just want you to know what you're up against. Casselli has a long memory, and he can be very patient. The downside is, he can be very *im*patient, too."

"Maybe I should have Mike's people get Marcel out of Rome and back to Paris."

"And how are you going to do that?"

"By reminding him how close he came to losing everything to the Russians last year."

"I don't think Marcel is accustomed to feeling vulnerable," Dino said. "Maybe you're underestimating him."

"I hope so," Stone said.

# 17

It was nearly lunchtime when Stone's new cell phone rang, and the caller ID number was blocked. "Hello?" he said cautiously, prepared to hang up again if it was Casselli.

"Stone, it's Lance," Lance Cabot said.

"Lance, how did you get this number?"

"And good day to you, too. Is there some reason I shouldn't have this number?"

"Yes, I've had it for no more than a couple of hours, and I got it for the specific reason that—"

"Yes, yes, I know about all of that. Mr. Casselli was making a pest of himself."

"Right, and if you can get the number, can't Casselli?"

"I very much doubt it—after all, I'm the director of fucking Central Intelligence, and I can get *any-*

*body's* number. I don't believe Leo Casselli can. Do you mind very much speaking to me?"

"Of course not, I'm just concerned that I was so easy to find."

"Oh, all right, when I got an out-of-order recording on your old number, I called your secretary, Joan, and she gave me the new one. I don't think she would give it to Casselli, so stop worrying."

"All right, I won't worry."

"Actually, perhaps you should worry just a little, because Casselli called you yesterday and was connected to your old number for a couple of seconds."

"Yes, I'm aware of that."

"That was long enough for him to get a fix on your general location, if he has the right equipment, and I'm sure he does, so you should assume he knows you're in Paris."

"Swell."

"But, if you hung up immediately, he probably doesn't have your street address."

"Well, that's a relief."

"Don't be relieved too quickly, he might have gotten it."

"Oh?"

"But don't worry, I've got a fix on Casselli's phone, and he's still in Rome."

"That's good to know."

"Of course, he may be sending his minions to Paris as we speak."

"I can't win, can I?"

"Of course, if they don't have your street address, they can't find you, can they?"

"It's always so reassuring to talk to you, Lance."

"I'm glad to hear it. I suppose you're wondering why I'm calling."

"That crossed my mind."

"Rick LaRose is going to come to see you." Rick was the Paris station chief for the Central Intelligence Agency.

"It's always a pleasure to see Rick."

"Not this time. He's going to ask you to do something you won't want to do."

"And what would that be?"

"I can't talk about it on the phone. Rick will explain it all when you see him."

"I can hardly wait."

"Don't be sarcastic, Stone, it doesn't suit you."

"Would you prefer irony?"

"That doesn't suit you, either."

"And what is Rick going to do for me, in return for my doing something for you that I won't want to do?"

"He's going to keep Casselli and his friends from capturing you and barbecuing you on a spit."

"Is that what Casselli wants to do to me?"

"He did that to someone very recently—last week, I think."

"You're just trying to frighten me."

"I am, because you should be frightened. Under Casselli's thin veneer of respectability, he's really a vile and barbaric creature. I wouldn't put anything past him. I could tell you stories from our file on him that would turn your hair white."

"Don't, please."

"If you're nice to Rick, I won't."

"I'll be as nice to him as I can be, under the circumstances."

"I was looking for a more unqualified response."

"That's the best I can do—under the circumstances."

"I suppose. I understand the new girl, Ms. Kiesler, is very nice."

"You know about her, too?"

"Stone, we've known each other for a long time—when are you going to get used to the fact that I know everything about everybody?"

"Never."

"Would you like me to tell you something about Ms. Kiesler that you don't know?"

"Thank you, no. I'd prefer to hear it from her."

"As you wish, but she may prefer to keep it from you."

"As she wishes."

"If your curiosity overwhelms you, call me."

"Goodbye, Lance."

"Goodbye, Stone."

# 18

Hedy took her easel back into the mews and set it up, while Stone returned to his book. He had been reading for no more than ten minutes when a chime chimed. It took Stone a moment to remember what rang the chime, then it came to him: it rang when somebody opened the door in the big gates. By the time he got to his feet, somebody was ringing the doorbell.

He opened the door to find Rick LaRose, as predicted. "Hello, Stone," Rick said, smiling and offering his hand.

"How did you get in?" Stone asked.

"I have a key," Rick replied. "Have you forgotten from whom you bought this house?"

He had bought it from the Paris station, which had formerly used it as a safe house. "How are things at the Paris station?" he asked as he offered Rick a chair.

"Fairly calm at the moment. It's one of those welcome periods where we're not in the middle of a flap of some sort."

"It sounds restful."

"Boring, is more like it."

"Lance said you are going to ask me to do something I won't want to do."

Rick looked a little embarrassed. "Well, yes. What's more, it's not something that I want to ask you to do."

"As bad as that?"

Rick shrugged.

"Are you just trying to make things less boring for yourself?"

"Oh, sure, but there's a real purpose in it, too. It's something that could help us make things materially better in Europe."

"Better for whom?"

"For Europeans."

"Okay, spit it out."

Rick was now looking sheepish. "We'd like you to let us leak your location to Leo Casselli."

Stone winced. "I don't think I could have heard you correctly, Rick."

"I'm afraid you did."

"Look, I've just fled Rome in order to get out of

Casselli's reach. How far do I have to go? London? Iceland? Home to New York?"

"It's like this," Rick said. "There's a guy in Rome, Massimo Bertelli, who has just taken over the DIA, the Italian department that is trying to root out the Mafia."

"I've heard the name," Stone said.

Rick looked surprised. "Where did you hear of him?"

"From Dino Bacchetti."

"Dino Bacchetti in New York?"

"Right now he's upstairs taking a nap."

"I didn't see him on the arrivals list," Rick said.

"Arrivals list?"

"Every day the embassy circulates a list of prominent Americans who are visiting France. Dino wasn't on it."

"It's a private visit," Stone said. "He's just here for the weekend, with his wife."

"Nevertheless, we like to know who's in town."

"Now you know. Dino has been in touch with Massimo Bertelli about Marcel duBois's and my problem with Casselli."

"Oh, good, that will save me the trouble of informing him."

"I guess so. Are you going to tell me what you— rather, what Lance—wants?"

"It's partly to do with an expansion of my job. The Agency wants station heads to be more concerned with what happens in Europe as a whole, rather than just in our individual bailiwicks. We're beginning to think of the European Union as more of a United States of Europe, rather than a lot of independent countries."

"Well, that's very cosmopolitan of the Agency, Rick, but what the hell does that have to do with me?"

"It's like this: France has some very comprehensive laws dealing with organized crime."

"Doesn't Italy?"

"Yes, but it's more difficult for the Italians to enforce them. The Mafia there has long penetrated government at every level. They're doing the best they can to root them out, but they have a lot of hurdles to overcome."

"Go on."

"Bertelli and his people have assembled intelligence indicating that Casselli wants to spread his influence to other European countries, especially France."

"Why France?"

"It boils down to the recently discovered fact that Casselli wants a personal base here. He particularly likes Paris, but the attitude of French law enforcement toward him would make it difficult for him to live here, even for short periods of time. He would like, over time, to penetrate French society and, eventually the civil service and the legislature, with an eye to making France more hospitable to him and his friends."

"That sounds megalomaniacal to me."

"Of course it does, but Casselli has a lot of confidence in his own ability to manipulate things."

"Once again, how does this affect me?"

"Casselli wants to co-opt people like Marcel and you, who do business here and who move from country to country easily. Casselli can't even visit Paris or London for fear that his name would be on some watch list that would get him detained at the airport."

"Why doesn't he just drive?"

"Of course that would be easier, if he were just visiting, say, for pleasure, but French hotels collect their guests' passports and send the names to the police every day, so eventually his name would cross the desk of some civil servant who is on the lookout for people like him, and he'd find himself dealing with the police and the court system."

"Come on, Rick, get to the point."

"We know that Casselli has agents in Paris already who are attempting to winnow their way into French society, but we have had trouble identifying them. Now, however, there is someone in Paris who is of great interest to them, someone who might coax them out of the woodwork and into the light, giving us a rare opportunity to identify them and penetrate their organization."

"And that would be me?"

"Yes."

"Sort of like the goat that would be staked out to attract the lion?"

"That's not a comparison we'd like to draw."

"Nevertheless, the comparison is apt, is it not?"

"Neither Lance nor I would be comfortable with that. We know that Casselli is doing his best to locate you—we just want to make it easier for him."

"Rick, you realize, do you not, that sometimes, in spite of the hunter's best efforts, the lion eats the goat?"

"All we want you to do, for the present, is to start using your old phone again."

"Just long enough for Casselli to deduce my street address in Paris."

"Well, yes. We'll take care of the rest, and we will, as we have done in the past, protect you."

Stone sighed. "I don't know why I don't just go back to Rome."

"Because in Rome, in spite of the Italians' best efforts, the lion would eventually get the goat."

# 19

S tone stared at Rick LaRose. "You want me to risk my life—and, incidentally, the life of my girlfriend, who is also here?"

"Stone, I've said we will protect you. There is little risk involved for either of you. Right now there are half a dozen of our people on the street and rooftops whose only purpose is to keep you safe. And right now, all Casselli knows is that you are in Paris, no more. And there's something else: for all practical purposes, this house doesn't exist."

"How is that?"

"When we owned the property we had it erased from all civic records—city directories, maps, even tax rolls. Have you ever received a bill for taxes for the house?"

"Joan normally takes care of those things, I'd have to ask her."

"Trust me, you haven't. And we sold the house, not to you, personally, but to a French corporate entity your attorneys created for the purpose, so your name does not appear in any list of property owners."

"Well, that's a high level of anonymity," Stone admitted, "and it could be very useful. I'm not sure I'd want to give that up. Are you going to notify the French authorities that this house exists?"

"Stone, if we wanted to force you to cooperate, we could just let Casselli know where you are. He would kill or kidnap you and we would follow his people to the source and erase him. But that's not how we deal with people we like and who are of value to us, as you have been on a number of occasions."

"I had no idea the Agency was so fond of me," Stone said wryly. "What do you want me to do?"

"Where is your old phone?"

Stone opened a drawer in the table next to him and handed Rick the phone.

"May I have your new phone?"

Stone removed it from its holster and handed it to him.

Rick removed the SIM card from the new phone

and installed it in the old phone, then handed it to Stone. "Why don't you check in with Joan, see how things are in New York?"

Stone called the number.

"Woodman & Weld," Joan said.

"It's Stone."

"Are you safely in Paris?"

"I am. Thank you for alerting Marie of our arrival. How are things in New York?"

"Under control. Strangely, it gets easier to keep it that way when you leave town."

"Dino and Viv are here for the weekend."

"Good for them. You seem to be rambling, Stone, is there something I can do for you?"

"Hold on a minute." Stone turned to Rick. "Is that long enough?"

"Give it another minute or two," Rick said.

Stone went back to the phone. "Any interesting mail?"

"Nope."

"Phone messages?"

"Nope."

"Oh, I know what I wanted to ask you: Have we ever received a bill for taxes for the Paris house?"

She thought about that. "Nope."

"Okay, then, call me if anything comes up. Oh, and if one phone doesn't answer, try the other one."

"Goodbye, Stone." She hung up.

"That should do it," Rick said. "Now, if Casselli's people traced the call, they'll get a marker on their map, but the marker won't correspond to any known Paris address, which will confuse them. But I would imagine that they would have people in the neighborhood within the next twenty-four hours, looking for you."

"And what happens when they find me?"

"We'll bag and interrogate them for a few days."

"Will Casselli know what's happened to them?"

"No, he'll just suddenly be out of touch, and he'll send more people to find them, and when he does, we'll bag and interrogate *them*."

Stone thought for a moment. "Suppose I could get Casselli to come to Paris? Would that shorten the project?"

"How would you get him to do that?"

Stone's cell phone rang. "I'll bet that's him now."

"Go ahead, see what you can do."

Stone pressed the button. "Hello?"

"Mr. Barrington?"

"Yes."

"This is Leonardo Casselli."

"Hello, Mr. Casselli, what can I do for you?"

# 20

Casselli seemed momentarily nonplussed, then he collected himself and spoke. "I think perhaps it would be useful if you and I met."

"Fine, how about lunch tomorrow?"

"I'm committed for that time. Would the day after tomorrow be convenient?"

"Brasserie Lipp, in Saint-Germain-des-Prés at one o'clock?"

"But that is in Paris," Casselli said.

"And I am in Paris," Stone replied. "I don't know when or if I'll be returning to Rome. I may have to go back to New York soon."

"Paris is awkward for me," Casselli said.

"All right, New York?"

"No," Casselli said. "Brasserie Lipp at one o'clock the day after tomorrow."

"I'll book," Stone replied. "See you then." He hung up and turned to Rick. "Day after tomorrow."

"I'm astonished," Rick said. "It can't be that easy."

"Apparently, Casselli thinks that dealing with me would be easier than dealing with Marcel. As you heard, I told him I wouldn't be returning to Rome."

"Then I'll get in touch with our French partners and arrange for him to be detained."

"Not until after lunch," Stone said.

"Why after?"

"Because I want to hear what he has to say. And I want to see if I can persuade him to leave us alone."

"Good luck with that," Rick said, standing up. "Now, I have a meeting at my office."

"Thank you for the protection," Stone said. "I feel better knowing your men are out there. If Hedy should leave the house, please see that she is followed."

"Of course," Rick said. They shook hands, and he departed.

Dino came downstairs, yawning. "What time is dinner?"

"Seven-thirty?"

"It's dinnertime in New York."

"No, it's lunchtime. Go see Marie in the kitchen—she'll find something for you."

Dino disappeared into the kitchen, and Hedy

came inside, carrying her easel. "I'm beginning to feel confined," she said.

"Try the roof," Stone replied. "There are some interesting views from up there."

"Good idea."

"Take the elevator to the top and walk up one flight. Don't be surprised if you encounter a man with a gun."

"Would he be theirs or ours?"

"Ours. Introduce yourself."

She vanished into the elevator, and Dino returned to the living room, bearing a sandwich and a beer.

"What's this called in French?" he asked, indicating the sandwich.

"*Croque-monsieur*. A grilled ham and cheese."

Dino took the chair next to Stone's and had a bite. "It tastes different from a ham and cheese at home."

"Lots of butter."

"I saw Rick LaRose leaving, didn't I?"

"You did. He and his people are watching over us."

"Well, that gives me a nice warm feeling inside."

"It's the *croque-monsieur*."

"Maybe you're right. What's new with Rick?"

"I think you already knew that he's the station chief in Paris?"

"I know."

"What's new is that the Agency, meaning Lance, is beginning to view the European community as one country, the United States of Europe."

"That's broad-minded of Lance. How will that help them do their job?"

"I think they're trying to find that out right now. Sounds great on paper, though, or at a congressional hearing."

"I never think of Lance reporting to anybody."

"Lance has a budget, like every other top bureaucrat, and it has to be approved by Congress."

"I suppose."

"Still, I think Lance manages to be more of an autocrat than most other Agency heads. Right now, he's taken the view that I should be a sacrificial goat in order to entrap Casselli, who is the lion in this scenario."

"Are you going along with that?"

"To the extent that I have to, if I want his and Rick's protection while I'm in Paris."

"What about Hedy? Is she a goat, too?"

"No, just an innocent bystander who's beginning to learn who she's involved with. I'm doing my best to make her feel safe."

"Is she safe?"

"I hope so."

# 21

They enjoyed a very fine dinner at Lasserre that evening and Dino and Viv got to bed early to help with their jet lag.

While Hedy was getting ready for bed—a process that took half an hour—Stone took the elevator to the top floor, then walked up to the roof with a flashlight.

He opened the door and called out, "Hello? Anybody there? It's Barrington."

"Step out the door," a voice said, from nearer than Stone had expected. He switched on his flashlight and walked outside. Another flashlight came on, pointed at his face. "Good evening, Mr. Barrington. What brings you up here tonight?"

"A little fresh air, and I like the view."

"Everything all right down below?"

"Everything's just fine, thanks. I hope I didn't startle you."

"No problem."

Stone took in the view, including the Eiffel Tower, for a few minutes, then went back downstairs and got into bed. Hedy came in and snuggled up. "Are we safe?"

"We are safe."

"Are we going to stay that way?"

"I'm working on it."

"Then I feel safe."

They made love for half an hour and fell asleep in each other's arms.

The following day was sunny, and they drove out to Versailles in the old Mercedes convertible that had been part of the deal when Stone bought the house. They toured the palace, then had lunch at a local restaurant, and when they got back late in the afternoon, Rick LaRose was waiting for them in a black SUV, parked inside the gate.

"What's up?" Stone asked.

"We picked up some chatter. Casselli is, apparently, going to show up tomorrow," Rick replied. "He plans to have lunch, then return to Rome."

"If I can reason with him, do you still want to bag him?"

"I'll have to ask Langley." That meant Lance.

"I'd like to try, anyway."

"I came over to brief you on tomorrow's lunch."

"So, brief me."

"We're going to have a significant presence in and around the restaurant, that is, we and the Paris police."

"Good."

"Also, we've had a word with the maître d' about seating arrangements. Any apparent entourage of your luncheon companion will be shunted upstairs."

"Good idea."

"I also want you to record your conversation."

"I don't mind doing that."

Rick handed him a small jeweler's box. "This is what you'll use."

Stone opened the box to find a small American flag pin. The red stripes were rubies, the white ones diamonds, and the blue field diamonds on a background of sapphires.

"Just put that in your buttonhole," Rick said. "No visible wires or batteries. As soon as you plug the pin into the little clamp that holds it on, it activates. It's good for about three hours, which should be plenty."

Stone put the pin back into the box and the box into his pocket. "Okay."

Rick handed him another box. "This goes into your left ear," he said.

Stone opened the box and found what appeared to be a lump of plastic. There was also a sort of tool with a hook on the end.

"Push it into the ear as far as it will go. To get it out, use the little hook."

Stone examined the thing carefully. "You'll be able to talk to me?"

"Only if I have suggestions. If you can lead him into an admission of a crime, that would be a nice bonus."

"I doubt he's going to pour his heart out to me."

"Maybe he'll brag."

"Who knows?"

"Exactly. If he does, encourage him."

"I'll do that."

"You might also encourage him to threaten you. That would be helpful to the French. Tomorrow, you won't see any of us. Just leave the house and walk down the street to Lipp."

"Okay."

"Do you want a weapon?"

"What would I do with it? Shoot him in the middle of a popular restaurant? I'd never get a table again."

"Lance says to be careful."

"Lance always says that. He doesn't really think I'll be exposed to harm, does he?"

"Lance always expects that. It's not a bad policy. One more thing: when you've wrapped up your lunch, don't leave the restaurant with him. Make an excuse to stay."

"Okay."

"Good luck."

"Will I need it?"

"We'll see."

# 22

At ten minutes before one Stone left the house and strolled down the few blocks to Brasserie Lipp, doing some light window-shopping along the way. The restaurant, a longtime hangout for people in the arts, had outside tables and a ground-floor dining room, plus an upstairs one where the tourists were invariably sent, to keep the main room open for regulars. Stone thought of it as Paris's answer to Elaine's, his old hangout in New York, until the death of Elaine.

The maître d' recognized him immediately. *"Bonjour, M'sieur Barrington."* The two shook hands. "Your guest has not yet arrived." He led Stone to a table against the wall, with a good view of the front door. Stone settled in and ordered a bottle of Perrier. "And please," he said to the waiter, "bring large glasses for the wine and pour generously." The man nodded and left.

He had not long to wait. Casselli appeared at the front door, apparently alone, then approached the maître d'. Two men then entered the front door. The maître d' escorted Casselli to Stone's table, while his assistant greeted the two men and, after a short argument, sent them upstairs.

Casselli apparently didn't notice. Stone stood to greet him, and they shook hands coolly.

"I hope you had a good flight," Stone said.

"I did," Casselli said. "How did you know I flew?"

"I assumed that driving or taking a train would be cumbersome."

"Quite right. How long have you been in Paris?"

"I'm sure you know," Stone replied. May as well cut through the niceties.

Menus were brought.

"What's good here?" Casselli asked.

"It's an Alsatian restaurant. Try the *choucroute*."

"And that is . . . ?"

"Assorted meats and sausage on a bed of sauerkraut."

Casselli turned up his nose. "Oh, all right, after all, when in . . . Paris."

Stone ordered the food and a bottle of red wine.

"Now," Casselli said, spreading his napkin in his lap. "If we may speak of business."

Stone nodded. "Of course."

"I realize that both you and Mr. duBois are not Italian, and you may not be fully aware of how business is done in Rome."

Stone shrugged.

"Accomplishing such an enterprise as building a hotel in the city is very complicated . . . and very Italian."

"I would expect nothing less."

"There are many, many permits issued by separate city departments which are required for building."

"As there are in Los Angeles and Paris, where we already have hotels."

"Oh, it is quite different in Rome," Casselli said with a little smile. "One must deal with different . . . personalities, and in different departments they do not always operate by the same rules. Personal intercession by a knowledgeable intermediary can save much more time and money than the cost of such services. Everything goes more smoothly with the help of a . . . consultant."

"I should imagine," Stone said drily.

"You must have a permit for the foundations, then for the structure, then the roof—electrical, plumbing, all sorts of things."

"'Twas ever thus, 'twill ever be."

"What?"

"Please go on."

"Our services extend even to supervising the building's workforce and that of subcontractors."

"Mr. Casselli—"

"Leonardo, please."

"Leonardo, perhaps you are not aware that we have obtained all the required permits so far with little trouble with the bureaucracy. We, in fact, have already employed . . . consultants . . . who are performing satisfactorily."

"Ah, but you have had a major fire, which complicates things."

"Not really. We have obtained a permit for clearing the ground and starting over." Stone didn't really know about these things, just the broad strokes, but he wanted to needle Casselli.

The food and wine arrived, and the waiter poured generous glasses. Stone raised his and took a sip. Casselli raised his and took a gulp.

"Sometimes," Casselli continued, "frequently even, accidents occur on a site, and new permits are required."

"Leonardo," Stone said, "let me pause you right there. Clearly, you have spent much of your life in New York, and perhaps even on the Lower East Side and Little Italy. What you are trying to explain, decorously, to me is just a new version of an old practice.

Someone throws a brick through the window of a small shop, then magically, his colleague appears to offer the owner protection from such outrages. A small weekly fee and no more bricks through the window: no more customers covered in broken glass, no more plate-glass windows replaced. It's a very old racket, and I must say, I'm surprised that you have not found newer, more profitable ways to earn a living."

Casselli reddened slightly, then smiled. "And I am surprised that you would think that we are not more modern in our approach. Oh, and the food is delicious—good choice."

"Thank you. If you will forgive me for interrupting, I think I should take a moment to tell you what you are up against."

"Up against?" Casselli asked, as if he had never heard of such a thing.

"In this instance, you are not dealing with a shopkeeper, but with Mr. duBois, possibly the richest man in Europe, and one with many, many business resources, and in my case with a person of considerable wealth and associations that are wide and deep. Perhaps you have heard of a company called Strategic Services?"

"Vaguely."

"They are the second largest security company in

the world, with offices in fifty cities, employing more than thirty thousand highly trained personnel and as many more contractors, many of whom are former Special Forces, Navy SEALs, FBI agents, and police officers, with all the training and capabilities that their experience can provide them. I am the second largest stockholder in that company and its chief attorney, and I can call upon their skills at any time and very quickly. Some of your men have already encountered these people and have come off badly in comparison.

"Secondly, there is me: perhaps you do not know that I am a former New York City police officer, and that my partner during those years is now the police commissioner of New York City, the most important police officer in the world, who is on close terms with his counterparts in Europe, including a Mr. Massimo Bertelli, who, as I'm sure you know, is head of the Italian DIA, which is responsible for pursuing 'consultants' who attempt to extort legitimate businesses. Mr. Bertelli, I should tell you, is taking a keen interest in the operations of Arrington Hotels in Rome, and especially in the building and permitting process, and a keen interest in you, personally, and in your operations and personnel.

"Finally, if I can say this without bragging, I am an informal adviser to the former president of the

United States and his wife, the current president, and their close friend, which helps in all sorts of ways, and I am also a consultant to the Central Intelligence Agency, which helps in all sorts of other ways.

"So, should you continue to press your 'services' upon us, you will find yourself swept by a tsunami of government and police attention to your every move. And should you think that you are sufficiently legally detached from your operations, you should know that we are in a position to offer multimillion-dollar rewards and new passports to anyone who might offer evidence of your criminal connections. When that happens, some of your associates might find it more profitable and safer to realign their loyalties."

Stone refilled their wineglasses, then locked eyes with Casselli, who was paler, now, and trembling with anger. "Am I making myself perfectly clear?"

"No one has *ever* spoken to me in that manner," he said, "and lived to tell about it."

"Leonardo," Stone said evenly, "perhaps you had better become accustomed to being spoken to in that manner, both in court and outside of it. It is time for you to retire from 'business' and enjoy your ill-gotten gains, before they are all taken from you and the flesh flayed from your bones, leaving you to the vultures."

The waiter appeared and offered them dessert.

"I must go to the men's room," Casselli said. "Please order me a double espresso."

Stone ordered two and watched the man disappear down the stairs toward the toilets. Shortly, he heard a police siren from somewhere outside.

Casselli had been gone ten minutes when Rick LaRose came in, sat down in his place, and began drinking his espresso.

"I didn't hear from you through my earpiece," Stone said, fishing the thing out with its hook.

"I thought you were doing very well without my help," Rick replied.

"Did you take him?"

"He had a car waiting outside the kitchen door—a Paris police car. He's gone."

# 23

Rick walked back to the house with Stone, and once inside he excused himself and went into the library to make phone calls. It was getting chilly, so Stone lit the fire. Finally, Rick returned and sank into an easy chair.

"What did Lance have to say?" Stone asked.

"Lance was not amused."

"Wasn't it a police operation?"

"It was ours, with police backup."

"Ah."

"Lance was incensed that you invoked not only the Agency, but the president."

"You *told* him that?"

"He listened to your recording."

"Swell."

"What do you think Casselli will do now?"

"Do?"

"I thought that when you decided to let loose at Casselli you might have given some thought to how he would react. Did you think he would just leave meekly and never darken your life again?"

"Frankly, I thought he would be in the Bastille by now. It's just around the corner from Lipp."

"I don't think the gendarmes relished the thought of chasing one of their own cars through the streets of Paris with lights flashing and sirens sounding. It would have made the evening news."

"Can't the Italian police pick him up at the other end?"

"Pick him up for what? He's not wanted in Italy, and you apparently forgot to get him to incriminate himself."

"I got mad, I guess."

"I especially liked the parts about the 'tsunami' and 'flaying of flesh off his bones.'"

"I'm glad you appreciated my performance."

"I should have given you a script."

"I probably wouldn't have followed it."

"I guess not. What are you going to do now?"

"Spend a few days here, I guess, then go back to Rome."

"Back to Rome?"

"Well, I can't abandon Marcel in the middle of all this, and Hedy needs to go back."

"May I suggest that you persuade Marcel to run his business from Paris, and that you and Hedy get your asses back to New York?"

"And anyway, I promised Casselli a tsunami."

"You mean that wasn't an empty threat?"

"Certainly not. We've got Bertelli on our side, and he's the key man in Italy. I'll talk to Marcel about posting a reward for Casselli's neck in a noose."

"You think that will work?"

"Why not? Italians like money as well as everybody else, maybe more. It might shake somebody loose."

"You might begin by getting Dino to ask Bertelli to do the things you've already told Casselli he was doing."

"I forgot about that, heat of the moment."

"And as long as you've mentioned the Agency and the president—you seemed to forget the FBI and the attorney general—you might give some thought to what help you can ask of them. After all, they're your 'very close friends.'"

Stone winced. "Who else has heard the recording?"

"The gendarmes, and they were *very* impressed."

Stone groaned.

"Don't worry, Lance has ordered me to destroy the recording."

"Thank God for small favors."

"It's a shame, really, my people at the station would have loved it."

"And you would have played it for them?"

"Absolutely. I have to think of morale—I may play it for them yet."

"You wouldn't."

"Why not? It would make you famous inside the Agency. I'll just e-mail it and click on the 'send all' button."

Stone held out a hand. "Give it to me."

"You're a civilian, you can't destroy government property, only a government official can do that."

Stone pointed at the fire. "Then do it here, in my civilian fireplace."

"I guess there's no regulation about that." Rick fished a SanDisk card out of a pocket and flipped it like a coin into the fireplace, where it melted and sizzled.

"Thank you," Stone said.

Rick got up to go. "How do you know that was the real card? We spies are a devious lot."

"Can a civilian shoot a government official?"

"If he wants to get into a whole lot of trouble."

"What if he doesn't care?"

"Save it for Casselli. And don't forget, you've humiliated him—he's mad now." Rick gave Stone a little wave and left.

# 24

S tone, Hedy, Dino, and Viv had dinner at a neighborhood restaurant, where Stone gave them a summary of his conversation with Casselli.

They listened in silence, then Dino spoke. "I guess I'd better get on the horn to Massimo Bertelli tomorrow morning and get him started doing the things you told Casselli he was already doing."

"You think he will cooperate to that extent? Isn't he afraid of his superiors, the Mafia, or both?"

"Neither. He has a direct line to the prime minister, and where the Mafia is concerned, he has more guts than brains. He'll do anything he can to press them."

"In that case, I'd appreciate it if you'd call him first thing in the morning."

"What else are you going to do to create the 'tsunami'?"

"I'm ashamed to say I don't know. I'm not about to call the president, and I don't think Lance is in a mood to spring to my assistance after hearing the recording of my meeting with Casselli."

"You can put your money where your mouth is."

"You mean offering a reward for Casselli's arrest and conviction?"

"Sure. I'm sure Marcel would pick up half of it, so if you offered, say, five million and a passport for Casselli's head, you might get a nibble from somebody who knows a lot, maybe even land a fish."

"I'll do that first thing tomorrow."

"By the way, where are you going to get the passport?"

"Can you ask Bertelli to back us up on that?"

"Sure. I think he'll help."

Stone paid the bill, and they walked home. No sooner had they entered the house, when his cell phone rang, from a blocked number. "Hello?"

"It's Holly. How are you?" Holly Barker was an old and good friend and sometime lover who had formerly run the CIA New York station and now was national security adviser to the president.

"Okay, I guess."

"How's Paris?"

"How'd you know I'm in Paris?"

"I saw your video with Casselli at Lipp, and I loved it!"

"*Video!* I thought it was only audio."

"Nope, and with three cameras, too. They cut it like a movie: a two-shot, then close-ups of both of you when you spoke."

"Oh, shit, Rick threw a SanDisk into my fireplace when he was here, and I thought that was it."

"Never trust anything a spy does."

"Never again. Please tell me this hasn't reached the president."

"It hasn't from me, but I'm sure by morning somebody in the Agency e-mail loop will have forwarded it to her. You might devote some time, though, to hoping it doesn't get leaked to some reporter."

Stone sighed. "I'm in very deep shit here. I ignored Rick's instructions and got the bit in my teeth. I'm never going to live this down."

"You will, if it helps you get Casselli. What are you doing about that?"

"Looking for ideas."

"You might ask President Kate to call the Italian prime minister and ask him to exert some downward pressure on Casselli through not just the DIA but all the other Italian police departments, of which there are many."

"I can't ask Kate to do that."

"You want me to ask her? I'm happy to do it. The worst she can say is no, and she might not say that."

"No, I'm too embarrassed at having used her as leverage, especially when I didn't have it."

"Whatever you say. I gotta run now. Call me if I can help in any way."

"Thanks, Holly, I really appreciate that, and if I get an idea, I'll call." They said goodbye and hung up.

"That was Holly," he said to Dino. "Turns out my audio had video attached."

"Sheesh!" Dino said, laughing. "You just get in deeper and deeper, don't you?"

"Tell me about it."

Stone's phone rang again. "Hello?"

"This is the White House operator. I have the president for you. Can you speak to her?"

Stone's heart sank. "Yes, thank you." He covered the phone and said, "It's Kate."

Dino burst out laughing.

"Hello, Stone?"

"Yes, Madam President?"

"I just *loved* your video."

Stone's heart leaped. "I didn't even know it was a video, until Holly called."

"That's right, she would already have seen it."

That meant that Holly hadn't spoken to Kate. He was relieved about that.

"How can I help?" Kate asked.

"Madam President, I am so sorry to have brought you into this. I—"

"Nonsense. You've done me so many favors, and I've done you so few. Please tell me how I can help."

"Well, we're getting good cooperation from Massimo Bertelli, who's head of the Italian DIA, but if you could call the prime minister, there's a whole array of Italian police departments that could be brought to bear, if he's serious about fighting the Mafia."

"What a good idea! What time is it over there?"

"It's a little after ten."

"I'll schedule a call to the PM for first thing tomorrow. Anything else?"

"If you could find a way to let Lance know that you're not angry with me, he might speak to me again someday."

"Done. I'll call him right now."

"Thank you so much for your help."

"What are friends for? See you." She hung up.

"What did she say?" Dino asked.

"She's going to call the PM in the morning. I may have a life again."

"So you're out of the shit."

"Maybe."

"You've got more than nine lives, pal."

"Friends are better than nine lives."

"I'll take that as a compliment."

"You certainly may."

Lance Cabot had fallen asleep with a mission report lying open on his chest when the phone rang. "Yes?"

"This is the White House operator. Can you speak with the president?"

This was going to be about the Stone Barrington thing, he knew it. "Of course."

"Hello, Lance?"

"Yes, Madam President?"

"Have you seen the video of Stone Barrington and the Italian mafioso Casselli?"

"Yes, ma'am, and I'd like to explain about that."

"Isn't it wonderful!"

Lance sucked in a breath and searched for words. "Stone is full of surprises, isn't he?" That avoided both criticism and endorsement.

"He really tore into him, didn't he? I talked with Stone a few minutes ago, and he needs our help. I'm going to call the Italian prime minister tomorrow morning and ask him to put his entire police force on Mafia alert and to make every effort to support Massimo Bertelli at the DIA."

"That's a wonderful idea, Madam President."

"It occurs to me that there must be things your people in Italy can do to support the effort and to help get the Mafia off Stone's and Marcel's backs. I've heard all about what's going on with their plans for a hotel in Rome."

"Well, the Mafia don't always come under our brief, Madam President."

"You didn't have any scruples about going after the Russian Mob in Paris last year, and I've never seen that in your brief. Would you like me to issue a presidential finding that would cover your ass?"

"Oh, madam, I don't think that would be necessary." He thought for a slim instant. "But if you have a moment to dictate something, it would be very helpful."

"I'll get it to you tomorrow, Lance. Now, you pull out all the stops, you hear?"

"Yes, ma'am."

"Good night, then."

"Good night, ma'am." He hung up the phone and found himself panting. Stone Barrington was going to be the death of him yet.

# 25

After rising the following morning Stone was in the library making notes for his call to Marcel when Dino came in with a bag of croissants and the *International New York Times*, formerly the *International Herald Tribune*.

"We've got some rethinking to do," Dino said, tossing the newspaper into his lap.

Stone put down his pad and picked up the paper. A large headline occupied the upper-right-hand corner of the front page:

## TOP ITALIAN MAFIA COP ASSASSINATED IN ROME

"It happened when he was driving home from work last night," Dino said. "He left the ministry with a driver in an armored Lancia. They were in rush hour traffic at a standstill, when a motorcycle pulled up beside them, and the guy on the backseat shoved a bomb under Massimo's car. Apparently, the car wasn't equipped to handle that. It blew about six feet into the air and broke in half. Massimo and his driver were both killed instantly." He picked up the remote control and turned on the TV. In a moment he had found the BBC News channel, and they watched the footage from a security camera in the street as it played and replayed the explosion.

They listened to the report for a few minutes, then the news reader heard something in her earpiece, and she was handed a sheet of paper. "This just in," she said. "Two top Italian Mafia leaders have this morning been gunned down almost simultaneously: one in Naples and one in Rome, the Italian DIA is reporting. Their names have not yet been released." She moved on to another story, and Dino switched off the TV.

"That's bad about Massimo," Stone said. "My condolences."

"He was a tough guy. I'm sorry they got to him before he got to them."

"Do you have any idea who his successor will be?"

"I'm hoping it will be his deputy, Dante Fiore. He's a good guy, too, and tough. What do you think about the two mafiosi who got it this morning?"

"What do you think?"

"I think Casselli has headed us off at the pass: he's knocked off his chief government pursuer, the guy that you threatened him with, and he's identified a couple of his cohorts that he thought might go for your reward, while sending a message to his other minions that defections will not be tolerated. The guy is some tactician."

Stone's phone rang. "Hello?"

"It's Holly. I suppose you've heard the news about Signor Bertelli's assassination?"

"Yes, I have. Dino and I just watched the explosion on the BBC. And did you hear that two top mafiosi were knocked off this morning?"

"Yeah. What does that mean?"

"We think it's a reaction by Casselli to my threat to post a reward on his head. Now he's eliminated the people he thought might be vulnerable to the reward and sent all his other people a message. He's smarter than I thought."

"Yeah, he must be. I just talked to President Kate, and she told me about your conversation last night. She did that on her own, not at my suggestion. She also called Lance and lit a fire under him, so you'll find the Italian station helpful, I expect."

"Could you get her a message from me before she makes the call to Italy?"

"Sure."

"Tell her that Dino, who knows the setup at the DIA, thinks Bertelli's deputy, Dante Fiore, is the man to replace him. He has a very high opinion of the guy."

"That's a good call," Holly said, "and she'll appreciate Dino's recommendation. She met both men when we were in Italy last year. I'm sure she'll be glad to mention Fiore to the PM."

"Thank her for me, will you?"

"Sure. Talk to you later." Holly hung up.

"Dino," Stone said, "why don't you see if you can get through to Dante Fiore and give him our condolences? Maybe we can get some fresh intel from him."

Dino sat down next to him, looked up a number in his iPhone, pressed the speaker button, and waited. "This is his direct line," he said.

*"Pronto,"* a vigorous voice said.

"Dante, it's Dino Bacchetti."

"Hello, Dino! Good to hear from you."

"I'm with my friend Stone Barrington, who Massimo may have told you about. We've just heard the news about Massimo, and we wanted to express our condolences."

"Thank you, Dino, that's very kind. I've been working this all night, and we're sure it's Casselli, though we can't yet prove it. My thanks to you, too, Stone. I'm aware of your problems with Casselli and your hotel project, and I want you to know we'll continue to watch over it."

"Thank you, Dante."

"By the way, I saw your video with Casselli early this morning, and I enjoyed it very much, seeing him squirm like that. You know about the two mafiosi in Naples and Rome who got hit this morning?"

"We just saw it on the BBC."

"We here think that's a result of your threat about the reward on your video, but even if nobody takes the reward, we've got two top guys out of the way, and that's a win for us. It doesn't replace Massimo, but it's a win, and we'll take all those we can get."

"Dante," Dino said, "I want you to know that Stone spoke to President Kate Lee last night. She's calling your PM along about now, and he sent her a message this morning, mentioning your name."

"That's very good of you, Stone. I'm not sure I dare hope for the job, but I'd love to do it. Hang on a minute." They could hear some muffled conversation, then Dante came back. "I've just had a message to see the PM in half an hour. I'll call you back, if there's anything new." They gave him Stone's number and let him go.

"Maybe you did some good this morning," Dino

said. "And maybe you're digging your way out of the shit."

"God, I hope so, I thought I had blown the whole thing to bits."

"Just Massimo and the two hoods, and my guess is that Casselli already had plans to hit Massimo. It didn't seem like an improvised attack."

Stone's phone rang again, and he reached out and pushed the speaker button. "Hello?"

"Stone, it's Lance."

"Good morning, Lance, you're up early."

"I didn't get much sleep last night. I've been on the phone with the Rome station, making preparations for your return."

# 26

S tone blinked. "My return?"

"We'd like you to go back to Rome to-morrow morning. I've spoken with Marcel duBois, and he's happy to have you and your girl as his guests in his apartment over his offices. If Dino and Viv want to go, there's room for them, too. I understand he has quite an establishment there. The building has already been secured by Strategic Services, and people from our Rome station will take an interest, too."

"Why do you want me back there?"

"Do you remember your conversation with Rick about the goat and the lion?"

"Ah, yes."

"Your girl doesn't have to share that experience. We'll do our best to protect her, if she goes back to

Rome, but if she leaves the duBois building, she'll be a target for kidnapping, or worse."

"I'll speak to her about that."

"When you fly to Ciampino tomorrow, flight-plan for a noon arrival. You'll be met on the ramp and directed to a secure hangar that we maintain there."

"Thank you, Lance."

"The head of our Rome station is Jim Lugano, a bilingual Italian American and a good man. He'll meet you at the hangar with a secure vehicle, and you can talk about dealing with Casselli on the way into the city."

"Fine."

"Your debacle at Lipp seems to have turned into something of an advantage—you were always lucky, Stone. Goodbye."

"Goodbye."

Marie came into the library with a tray of Dino's croissants, butter, jam, and coffee, followed shortly by Hedy and Viv. Everybody said good morning, sat down, and dug into the pastries.

After breakfast, Dino stood up and beckoned to Viv. "We're going to take a little walk," he said. "We'll talk more when we get back." They left.

"I have a feeling we've been left alone for a talk," Hedy said.

"Right. I have to go back to Rome tomorrow, and

the best advice I can get is that you shouldn't return to the city."

She started to protest, but he held up a hand. "I'm moving into Marcel duBois's apartment above his offices, and if you come you'll be a virtual prisoner there. It's thought by thoughtful people that in Rome you would be a target for kidnapping."

Hedy made a gulping sound.

"Let me propose two alternatives: you can return to New York, or you can stay here, in this house, and paint. In either case, I'll have the Rome apartment cleaned out and your things returned to New York, and I'll take care of the rental charges there."

She thought about it for a moment. "Well, if I can't go with you, I think I'd prefer to stay in Paris and paint."

"Casselli is tracking my phone, so tomorrow he'll know that I've left Paris. Please wait until noon tomorrow, when I'll be back in Rome, before you leave the house alone. I'll ask Rick LaRose to have an eye kept on you, though you won't be aware of it."

She came over, sat in his lap, and kissed him. "Thank you," she said.

\* \* \*

D ino and Viv came back a few minutes later. "We've both talked with our offices, and we're going back to Rome with you. Viv is going to work with Mike Freeman on security there, and the mayor is going to let me take a few days for consultation with the Rome police on coordinating their operation against Casselli. While we were out, Dante Fiore called. The Italian prime minister has appointed him as Massimo's replacement. The announcement will be made this afternoon."

"That's good news."

"He tells me that the killing of Massimo and the phone call from the president to the Italian PM have helped concentrate the minds of the government, and maybe even the legislature, when it comes to measures to deal with the Mafia there. That can only be a good thing."

"How much do you know about how the Italians have been dealing with their Mafia?"

"Only what Massimo told me in a meeting in New York and in a few phone calls. These were about his plans, and not enough time has passed for them to have taken effect, so they'll be starting from scratch with Dante, albeit with Massimo's outline for his plans. Dante is going to ride in with us from the airport tomorrow, so he can tell us what his first moves are going to be."

"The head of the Agency's Rome station will be with us, too. His name is Jim Lugano, and I expect he already knows Dante."

"Maybe you'll get your tsunami after all," Dino said.

# 27

S tone lined up on the runway at Ciampino and set the CJ3+ down gently. As he turned off the runway a cart turned into his path with a flashing sign on the back saying: "Follow Me." Stone did so, and a lineman directed him to park in front of a large hangar. A large black Mercedes van pulled up to the airplane and waited. Stone saw two uniformed Italian policemen carrying automatic weapons standing guard at the van.

Stone, Dino, and Viv deplaned and retrieved their luggage from the airplane, then Stone locked it and got into the Mercedes with the others. The large compartment was set up as a conference table, and introductions were made. Jim Lugano was tall, thin, black-haired, and appeared to be in his early forties. He sported a dense mustache and was dressed in an obviously Italian suit. Dante Fiore was a solidly built six-footer with a thick neck and broad shoulders with short black hair. He pumped Stone's hand and welcomed him back to Rome.

"I hope your visit will be more peaceful than your last," he said. "And let me say, I'm glad your girlfriend chose to remain in Paris. We were not looking forward to protecting her while she painted in Rome."

"You are very well informed," Stone replied.

Dante took immediate control of their meeting. "I have spent two hours today meeting with the heads of half a dozen police divisions, and now each of them is back in his office, plotting with his staff to see how many ways they can harass the Casselli family and the others. Here are a few things we are already doing. One, vehicles identified as belonging to the families and their associates will be routinely followed and many of them stopped by the police for an examination of the vehicles and their documentation. Minor traffic and document infractions will be punished. Two, all known Mafia members with the rank of *capo* and above will be surveilled, with no attempt to hide our attentions. We want them to feel harassed. Warrants are being prepared to tap the telephones of those key men that are not already tapped, and noises will be made on the lines to let them know we're listening. And, of course, you will be glad to know, Stone, that we have posted large notices in certain neighborhoods in Naples and Rome that a five-million-euro reward and a new passport and resettlement help is being offered to anyone with information that can put Casselli in prison."

"Euros?" Stone asked. "Not dollars?"

"The euro is our currency."

"Oh, never mind, Mr. duBois and I will find a way."

Dino seemed to be suppressing a laugh.

"And we have placed uniformed policemen on the site of your hotel construction to protect it from criminal vandalism."

"Why," Stone asked, "are you going out of your way to let these people know they're being surveilled?"

"Because they have such a sense of entitlement over many years that they believe themselves invulnerable to law enforcement. We want to show them that is no longer so, unsettle them and make them nervous, because when they are nervous they will make mistakes. Casselli, for instance, has already had two of his most trusted associates murdered since your luncheon with him. Unfortunately, one of them has turned out to be already helping us, but the other has been a thorn in our flesh for years. We expect that now anyone who Casselli has the slightest reason to doubt will meet with the same fate.

"The tax authorities are also undertaking extensive audits of Casselli's legitimate businesses, as well as others thought to be part of his empire. Before today is out, a factory surreptitiously owned by him which produces olive oil falsely labeled as extra virgin will be shut down by the health authorities. A network of used-car lots owned by one of his associates and thought to be dealing in stolen vehicles will have each vehicle examined for signs of theft or lack of proper documentation, and if even one is found, the lot offering it for sale will be shut down and its inventory confiscated."

"That is all very encouraging," Dino said.

Jim Lugano spoke up. "Dante, we have facilities that may be useful to you in analyzing the wreck of Massimo's car for tracing the origins of bomb fragments, and they are available to you. We are also pressing those of our assets in the country who might be able to offer intelligence to report anything of interest.

"Dino, you are the guest of the Italian police, and they will be responsible for your personal safety, but our station will work with Strategic Services to protect Stone and Vivian. Our director was insistent on that."

"Thank you," Stone replied.

"Is there any other way we can be of service while you're in Rome?" Lugano asked.

"I'll think about it and let you know."

Lugano gave him a card. "These are all my numbers. I already have yours. Incidentally, I've been told that a while back you lost an airplane to a bomb in England."

"That is so."

"Our hangar at Ciampino is very secure, so you may rest easy about that. In any case, before you decide to depart, I will have your aircraft thoroughly inspected."

"Thank you."

T he courtyard at Marcel's offices was guarded by uniformed policemen, as well as Mike Freeman's personnel, in their dark suits. Marcel greeted them at the door and escorted them upstairs to their suites in his apartment.

He took Stone aside. "I have never seen such a surge of security in all my years," he said. "I have been to the building site this morning, and it is ringed by policemen. Oh, and Stone, I must tell you how much I enjoyed the video of your luncheon with Casselli."

Stone threw up his hands. "Is there anyone on the planet who hasn't seen it yet? Next thing I know, it will be showing in cinemas!"

Stone's cell phone rang. "Hello?"

"It's Hedy."

"Oh, hi, we just got to Marcel's offices. You okay?"

"I'm fine. I went out and did some grocery shopping early this morning, so I'm settled in."

"Hedy, I asked you not to leave the house until noon today, do you remember that?"

"But why?"

"I thought I explained it: Casselli is tracking my cell phone, and as soon as he sees that I'm in Rome, you'd be safer. Have you spotted any of Rick LaRose's people around you?"

"No, and the people on the roof are gone, too."

Stone heard a loud noise at her end of the phone. "What was that?"

"I don't know. Oh, somebody is kicking at the front door."

Stone thought fast. "Hedy, hang up and hide your cell phone in your crotch, and silence it. Hang on to it at all costs."

"Stone, they're going to get in!"

"Hang up and hide your phone in your crotch RIGHT NOW! We can trace you with it!"

The line disconnected, and all was quiet.

Stone called Rick LaRose.

"Yes?"

"It's Stone. Somebody is breaking into my Paris house as we speak. I think Casselli's people are taking Hedy."

"I've just tried to reach the man on her, and I'm getting no reply."

"I told her to hide her cell phone in her crotch—you can use it to trace her." Stone gave him the number.

"I've just heard: my man on Hedy was found unconscious by his relief man. He's on the way to the hospital. I'll trace Hedy."

"And cover Le Bourget. They may be trying to fly her here. I'll get this end covered. Call me with news." Stone hung up, found Jim Lugano's card, and called his mobile.

"Lugano."

"Jim, it looks as though my girl, Hedy Kiesler, has been taken from my Paris house. I've notified Rick LaRose, and he's covering Le Bourget, in case they try to move her here. I'd appreciate it, since you have a presence at Ciampino, if you'd cover that end.

We've got to try to get her back before they have a chance to spirit her off to Naples or somewhere else." He told Lugano about her cell phone and gave him the number.

"I'm on it, Stone. I'll be in touch."

Stone hung up the phone with a sinking heart. He had no doubt that Casselli would kill her or worse, if he felt like it.

Dino came over. "Your face is white. What's wrong?"

"It looks as though Casselli's people have taken Hedy from the Paris house."

"Oh, shit."

"I told her not to go out until I reached Rome, but she went grocery shopping this morning. Rick's man who was on her is down." He told Dino about her cell phone.

"That was a smart move," Dino said.

"I hope to God they don't find it," Stone replied, and he meant it.

# 28

Rick LaRose pressed a button on his phone that rang a dozen other phones, the users of which punched on and waited for instructions.

"This is a Mayday," Rick said into the phone, "this is not a drill. Our surveillance subject, one Hedy Eva Marie Kiesler, has been taken from the Barrington house in Saint-Germain. I want a full-blown alert in the neighborhood, and team one to Le Bourget, all FBOs covered, *now*. I want a list of every aircraft taking off from that airport today, whether a flight plan is filed or not, its destination and time en route, with particular attention paid to flights to Italy or near the border. All teams: she's probably in the trunk of a car or in the back of a van, and that will be tough. Use firearms as necessary, but be careful. Any questions?"

No one spoke. Rick hung up and called Jim Lugano and told him what he'd done.

"We've already got Ciampino covered," Lugano said, "and we're extending to the other Rome and Naples airports as we speak."

"I'm going to ask the French to do vehicle checks of suspicious cars and trucks at the French/Swiss border," Rick said.

"I'll do the same at the Swiss/Italian border," Jim responded.

"Our confidence is not high," Rick said.

"Neither is ours."

"Avoid telling Stone that, until we know more."

"Right." Both men hung up.

S tone had a progress report from both men; no trace of the cell phone. He hung up and stared out the window.

"You know the chances of getting her back are slim," Dino said.

"Casselli will respond to money," Stone replied. "I'll ransom her back, no matter what it takes."

"Stone, Casselli didn't do this for money, his motives are two: leverage or revenge—or both. What happens to her is going to be decided by which is more important to him."

Stone knew that Dino was right, but he couldn't bring himself to agree with him.

"Now we wait," Dino said. "They'll be in touch."

"Or they'll dump her body somewhere they know we'll find it."

"There is that. We'll do better at this if we try to remain optimistic."

"I'll try. It bothers me that we're not getting anything on her cell phone. Would they have searched her that carefully?"

Viv spoke up for the first time. "They will, but if Hedy's smart, the phone is not just in her underwear." She walked out of the room before they could respond; two minutes later, she was back.

"If Hedy's smart," Viv said, "the phone is inside her. I tried it—it's uncomfortable, but it works."

"Good going, Viv," Dino said, beaming at her.

"Her hands will be tied behind her back," Viv said. "She'll just have to relax until they reach their destination and cut her loose. Then we may get a signal. Stone, shouldn't you think about notifying her family?"

"Jesus, I hadn't even thought of that. Her stepfather, Arthur Steele, is a client of mine."

"He should be notified," Viv said. "It's possible that they may go to him for ransom, if they find out who Hedy is."

"How would they find out?"

"If they got her handbag, she may have the name in her passport as a person to notify. Steele is a very prominent American businessman. Casselli may even know who he is."

Stone sighed and got out his phone. He checked his watch: it was mid-morning in New York. He pressed the button on the contact.

"Mr. Steele's office," a woman said.

"This is Stone Barrington. May I speak to Mr. Steele, please?"

"Hello, Stone."

"Hello, Arthur. Have you heard from your step-daughter recently?"

"If you mean, do I know she's been seeing a lot of you, yes. Her mother had a note."

"Arthur, I have some difficult news."

"Is she dead?" He was alarmed.

"No, I have no reason to think that. We believe she's been kidnapped in Paris."

"By whom, and what was she doing in Paris? We thought she was in Rome."

"She was, but I found it necessary to leave Rome, and I thought she should come with me. I'm back in

Rome, but I thought it safer for her to remain at my house in Paris."

"Safer from whom?"

"Marcel duBois and I are building a new Arrington Hotel in Rome, and the local Mafia have made attempts to extort us to pave the way. We've resisted and have earned the enmity of the Italian Mafia chief, a man named Leo Casselli."

"I remember that name. Didn't he used to be in New York?"

"He had to leave the country, and he returned here."

"But why would he want to kidnap Hedy?"

"In order to put pressure on me to accede to his demands."

"This is all very confusing, Stone."

"Arthur, I want you to know that the relevant law enforcement agencies in both countries are working hard on this, and so is the United States government. They are pulling out all stops to recover Hedy and will continue to do so. I'm monitoring the situation on a minute-by-minute basis from Rome. If they demand a ransom, I will pay it."

"Stone, I know you well enough to know that you would not have deliberately placed Hedy in harm's way, and her mother and I, once I have explained things to her, will trust your judgment as to how to handle it. I would appreciate being kept informed, of course, but if you have to make any quick decisions, to help Hedy, please do so, and be assured of our support."

"That's very good of you, Arthur, and I'll do everything I can to help her and return her to her mother and you safely. In the meantime, I'll call you at least daily."

The two men said goodbye and hung up.

"How did he take it?" Dino asked.

"Better than I could have expected," Stone replied. "Arthur is not an excitable man. He remained cool. Who knows, that could change if things get worse. At any rate, I'm glad I'm dealing with Arthur and not her mother. I'm not sure I could handle that."

"Listen, pal," Dino said, "you're doing as much as anybody could in the circumstances."

"It reassures me to know you think so, Dino."

# 29

Hedy woke up on a blanket in what felt like the trunk of a car. Her hands and feet were tied, and she was blindfolded and gagged. She remembered the door being kicked in and the struggle but not much after that; she assumed she had been drugged. She had been stupid, leaving the house early to go to the grocery, instead of following Stone's instructions. She wondered what had happened to whoever was supposed to be following her.

The car came to a stop, and she heard the trunk lid unlatch. A man's voice, heavily accented, said, "You want toilet?"

"Yes," she said, and he hustled her to her feet and dragged her across a floor. "You'll need to untie my hands," she said.

He did so. He set her down on a toilet seat. "You got two minutes."

"Close the door, please."

To her surprise he did so. She got her jeans and underwear down and retrieved her cell phone, then while she peed, she lifted a corner of her blindfold, went to her contacts, and pressed the speed-dial button for Stone's number. Busy signal. Shit! She texted him: *I'm okay but—*

The man hammered on the door. "Time up."

She replaced the phone, got dressed, stood up, adjusted her blindfold, and groped for the doorknob. The door opened, knocking her back onto the toilet. "Thank you," she said. "I'm not going to scream. Please don't gag me again, I can't breathe well through my nose."

He didn't, but he retied her hands in front of her and threw her over a shoulder. She was carried a few yards, then up some stairs and dumped into a seat. A safety belt was fastened around her, and a moment later she heard a door being slammed shut. She assumed she was on an airplane. A moment later the airplane began to move slowly. She realized that she was in a hangar, and that the aircraft was being towed outside. She felt warm sun on her face.

An engine whined to a start. A jet, or maybe a turboprop; she knew the difference. Then a second engine. Someone put a headset over her ears, but it didn't seem connected to anything; she couldn't hear voices now, but the noise of the engines was muted to a whisper. One of those electronic headsets. She wriggled a bit in her seat. Snug. Not a big airplane like a Gulfstream; she had ridden in her stepfather's. A smaller airplane, maybe like Stone's. A Cessna, or a King Air, maybe. Someone plugged the headset into a socket, and she heard classical music: Mozart. It was pleasant.

The airplane began to move again, this time under its own power. It taxied for what seemed a very long time. A big airport? She decided it was a jet, not a turboprop. Less noise. Then it stopped again for some time. Finally it moved and turned and she felt pressed back into her seat with acceleration. The airplane was taking off. After a while it seemed to level off, and she dozed.

S tone's cell phone vibrated. He retrieved it, turned it on, and saw Hedy's message: *I'm okay but—*

"Contact!"

Dino, who had been dozing in his chair, sat up. "What contact?"

"She tried to send a message but was interrupted, just said she was okay, *but*."

"But she's been kidnapped."

"Exactly, but she has access to her cell phone."

"They must have let her go to the toilet," Viv said, "but they didn't give her much time."

"You were right, Viv," Stone said.

"It seems so."

Stone texted back. *I hear you. Try again when you can.*

Hedy didn't wake up until the plane touched down. She pretended still to sleep. There was more taxiing, then the plane stopped, then was towed again, this time for a longer ride. Finally, her headset was removed, her seat belt unbuckled, and she was hoisted to her feet and slung over a shoulder again. Men were speaking in Italian, which she understood. She resolved to speak and respond to only English. It might give her some sort of edge. Shortly, she was placed in another car trunk, and the car drove away. Although her hands were now tied in front of her, she made no attempt to reach her cell phone again, because she didn't know how long she would have before she was interrupted, and she didn't want to lose the cell phone. She dozed again, and when she woke, she didn't know how long she had been out. She must still have some of the drug in her. Now they were driving more slowly and making very sharp turns in both directions.

Hedy remembered a road like this: the Amalfi Coast. After an hour or so the car came to a stop, and doors opened and slammed. She was taken out of the trunk again and slung over what felt like the same shoulder. There were steel-like clangings, and she felt the gravity increase and heard the whine of machinery. An elevator, probably some sort of industrial one, hence the louder-than-usual noise as they climbed.

They climbed for what seemed a long time.

# 30

Jim Lugano answered his cell phone. "Lugano."

"It's Lance. What news of the girl?"

"Stone called, he's had a partial text. She said she's all right, but she was cut short. She's a smart girl, apparently, she's hidden her phone."

"Smart indeed. Why haven't we bagged these people? Couldn't her position be nailed from the call?"

"Not enough time. We don't yet know how they're traveling. I hope they're not in a car or truck, that would make it much more difficult. Rick has expanded his airport survey to every airport inside of fifty miles of Paris. We're doing the same in Rome and Naples, but they could have landed anywhere—in a field, if they have the right plane—and switched to a vehicle. Confidence is not high."

"I don't like hearing that."

"I don't like feeling it."

"Have the girl's family been contacted?"

"Stone spoke to her stepfather, who turns out to be Arthur Steele, of insurance fame."

"That makes me wonder why I haven't heard from a senator or two."

"He apparently has enough confidence in Stone to let him handle it."

"Or enough indifference not to care much what happens to the girl."

"I don't think that. She has a mother he has to live with."

"What's our best hope, given what we know?"

"Another cell call or text, on the air long enough for us to locate. We don't know how much cell reception she has at her destination, wherever that is, or how much of a charge she has left on the phone. It's going to be dodgy."

"Everything is always dodgy," Lance said. "Keep in touch." He hung up.

S tone looked up and was surprised to see Mike Freeman stride into Marcel's living room. "What brings you across the Atlantic?" he asked.

"My two most important clients and my insurer's daughter," Mike said, sinking into a chair. A butler approached and inquired of everyone's refreshment choices. A bottle of San Pellegrino satisfied them all.

Stone brought Mike up to date on the text message and Viv's theory on where the phone was housed.

"Smart girl," Mike said. "Stone, is she smart enough to keep her cool until we find her?"

"I think she's already shown us that. I've sent her a text, so the next time she's able to check the phone, she'll know we're looking for her. I hope we'll get more information, too."

"I hope she's doesn't end up in some remote farmhouse with no cell reception," Mike said.

"I hadn't thought of that. I guess I just take reception for granted, and I shouldn't in this case."

"It's a thickly enough populated country to give us hope."

Hedy woke up in a darkened room. She let her eyes become accustomed, then had a look around. She was no longer blindfolded but her hands and feet were tied. She was on a single bed in a small room, like a maid's room. She spied a door ajar and hopped over to it, finding a small bathroom. She got her jeans down, retrieved the phone, and peed. She switched on the phone and got one dot of reception, on and off. She tried Stone's number but couldn't get through. She had less than fifty percent charge left. Why hadn't she charged it last night? Stupid!

She composed a text message, in the hope that it might eventually get through: *car, jet plane, car, windy road, A coast? Noisy elevator, high floor, small room, half battery, one dot. text back.* She got back to the bed; she tucked the phone between the mattress and box spring. Then she slept again.

S tone felt his phone go off and checked for calls and messages. Nothing. It vibrated again but still nothing. Then the message. "Okay, everybody," he announced, "Hedy has gotten through: she was put into a car, then a jet plane, then a car. She was on a windy road, maybe a coast, then had a long ride in a noisy elevator. She's in a small room, half her battery is gone, and she has one dot of reception."

"She's not going to get a call out with one dot," Mike said.

"The text seemed to take a couple of tries to get through."

Stone's phone rang.

"We got the message," Lugano said, "but texts go out so fast we couldn't nail even a general location, and Italy is mostly coast. Also, is 'windy' a winding road or one with a lot of wind? Either way, sounds like a coast road."

"She may not even be in Italy," Stone said. "She could be anywhere."

"Sounds like a skyscraper under construction on a coast," Dino said.

"Why do you say that?"

"Noisy elevator, maybe a construction site. You know those temporary elevators they throw up with scaffolding on the outside of a building under construction? Maybe an office building or a condo on the coast somewhere."

"I wish she could be more specific," Mike said.

"She's told us everything she knows," Stone remarked. "She's doing her best."

"Not good enough," Dino said. "Not yet, anyway."

# 31

Stone slept surprisingly well that night. Hedy was safe, and didn't sound abused, and that gave him some comfort. On the other hand, it was maddening to hear from her and get so little information. He joined the others for breakfast, and Mike Freeman was there, too.

"Where are you staying, Mike?"

"At my office. There's a little apartment there. Any messages from Hedy this morning?"

"Nothing—she probably slept."

"I have a chopper available, and a hospital bed for her the minute we get her back," Mike said.

"That's good thinking."

"I've had some research done on Casselli's past, by our staff psychologist," Mike said. "God knows, he's ruthless, but our man doesn't think he'll hurt or kill Hedy."

"I guess that's good news."

"The key seems to be, he's pragmatic and seems unlikely to act so much from spite as from need, and he doesn't need to harm her."

"Makes sense."

Jim Lugano turned up with some satellite photographs. "Here's Casselli's house on the Amalfi Coast," he said, laying an enlargement on the dining table.

"No outside elevator necessary," Stone said, pointing at the road to the house. "It's drivable."

"No signs of life there, and it's the only house there owned by Casselli. He could be anywhere, but I would think he'd feel safer in Naples than anywhere else. It's his home base, and he probably is more likely to have made inroads into the police there."

"Is there any building in Naples that might jibe with the description of Hedy's elevator ride?"

Jim got out his phone. "I'll find out." He punched in a number. "It's Lugano. I want a survey of the coast in Naples, to identify a tall building under construction with a temporary elevator, perhaps a condo, hotel, or office building. We have a kidnapping victim who has furnished us with such a description, and it is imperative that we locate her soonest.

Got it? Get back to me today." He hung up. "We're on it."

"I'd like to know where Casselli is," Stone said. "He might visit her."

"We haven't had eyes on Casselli since he left Lipp, in Paris."

"Can you please locate him? It seems to me that would be useful information."

"You're right." Jim got on his phone again and started issuing orders.

"I understand Casselli disposed of two of his closest people, for fear that they might be in touch with the police."

"Correct."

"I'd like to know who replaced them in his hierarchy," Stone said, "and if they're under surveillance. If Casselli isn't seeing Hedy himself, then somebody is taking care of her, and I think we should try and find out who that is."

"I don't think we have enough information right now to figure that out," Jim said. "If we could get a cell phone location, it would help."

"If we got a cell phone location, we would have most of what we need," Stone replied. "What are your capabilities when dealing with Casselli?" he asked. "What is authorized?"

"You mean, can we kill him?"

"Now that you mention it."

"That's a little steep at this stage of the game," Jim said.

"If we could kill him, he wouldn't be a problem anymore."

Jim laughed. "I can't argue with that, but I have not been authorized to kill him."

"Seek authorization."

Jim laughed again. "Jesus, Stone, I didn't know you were so bloodthirsty."

"I want my friend back, and I don't care if Casselli has to die in order to achieve that."

"To tell you the truth, I don't much care if he has to die, either. He's just interfering with our regular work."

"Ask Lance. Ask somebody."

J im excused himself, left the room, and called Lance. "This is Cabot."

"I've just been having a chat with Stone Barrington. He wants me to kill Leo Casselli."

Lance burst out laughing. "Is that all? Just bump him off? Who does he think we are?"

"Lance," Jim said, "Stone has a point."

"You mean you're happy to eliminate Casselli? Is that how you think we behave?"

"It wouldn't be the first time."

"Well, yes, but that sort of thing usually calls for a presidential finding."

"Usually, but not always. Casselli could have an accident."

"What did you have in mind?"

"Maybe the sort of thing these guys use to take each other out—his car nudged over a cliff, a bomb under his seat, a bullet to the head. After all, Casselli has just erased two of his top lieutenants, because he's afraid they might be talking to the police. There are surely those who might think that calls for a response. They must have family members or friends who might hold a grudge. If Casselli died, assumptions would be made about who did it and why, and I don't think we would rank high on anybody's list of possible perpetrators. If you need a bureaucratic reason, he's keeping us from our usual work."

"I like that. Do you know where he is?"

"Not yet, but I've issued orders to find him."

"Talk to me again when you have a location and a more definite suggestion for a plan."

"Right." Jim hung up and went back into the living room.

"Well?" Stone asked.

"It's being discussed."

# 32

ino came into the room. "I'm getting cabin fever," he said. "Let's go for a drive."

"We don't have a car," Stone replied.

"I can arrange that," Jim Lugano said, "and I'll provide security." He got on the phone.

Stone and Dino rode down in the elevator.

"You've been awful quiet, for you," Dino said.

"I'm thinking."

"Thinking about what?"

"About killing Casselli."

Dino laughed. "And how are you going to manage that?"

"Just find out where he is and kill him."

"Don't the police or the CIA know where he is?"

"Apparently not—their best guess is Naples."

"There are probably people better qualified than

you to take him out. You've never assassinated any-body, have you?"

"There's a first time for everything. I asked Jim to put it to Lance."

"What'd he say?"

"He didn't say no."

They were greeted downstairs by three of Lugano's people, one of whom handed Dino the keys to a Fiat sedan. "Be careful," he said, "the car's been tuned up."

"Great," Dino said. "Let's go do donuts in the Piazza del Popolo."

"Cars are now banned from the Piazza del Po-polo," the man said. "If you want to throw it around, go to the country and find yourself a nice field. Oh, by the way, it's armored, and it will take an IED, if it has to. Are you armed?"

"I am," Dino replied. "Stone?"

"No."

"What would you like?"

"Have you got a smallish .45?"

"How about model 1911 officer's?"

"That'll do."

The man went to the trunk of another car and came back with the pistol and a holster. Stone slipped it onto his belt, crossdrew, popped the magazine, shoved it back in, racked the slide, and put the safety on. He was handed two spare loaded magazines.

"Where are you headed?" the agent asked.

"Wherever we like," Dino said, getting behind the wheel and starting the car.

The agent handed him a handheld radio. "It's tuned to channel one. That'll keep you in touch with the following car."

Stone got in beside him, adjusted the seat, and put his spare magazines in the glove compartment. "Let's go."

"Where?"

"How about Naples?"

"Okay, I guess it's an hour on the autostrada." Dino handed Stone the radio, then punched Naples into the GPS and drove out of the courtyard.

A n hour later they were approaching Naples. "Anyplace special?" Dino asked.

"Keep to the coast as much as possible."

"What are we looking for?"

"A tall building under construction with a construction elevator. Oh, and if you see Leo Casselli, let's stop and shoot him."

"Anything we should watch out for?"

"I think Casselli likes big black Lancias."

They drove slowly along the coast, passing the

ferry terminal for the Isle of Capri. Dino stopped the car and pointed. "There," he said.

Stone turned and saw the skeleton of a building, maybe thirty stories. A mass of yellow scaffolding ran up one side.

"Like that?" Dino said.

"Something further along in construction," Stone said. "That one doesn't have any walls."

Dino continued driving, then after a few minutes stopped again. "Nearly finished," he said, pointing.

Stone looked at the building. "They've taken down the construction elevator and started using the interior ones. Too finished."

They drove on. After a while Dino said, "We've pretty much circumnavigated Naples, and no building fits the description."

Stone pointed. They were on the north side of Naples, driving along the water, and on the other side of the road, lit by the setting sun, was a tall building, apparently under construction, that had been enclosed but still had a construction elevator attached to one side. "What about that?" Stone said.

"Looks good to me," Dino said.

# 33

Dino pulled the car off the road and into the construction site, which was unfenced, wide open. It was getting dark.

Stone leaned forward and looked up. "There are lights on at the top," he said.

They got out of the car and were met by the two young men from the car behind them. "You think this is it?" one of them asked.

"It fits the description," Stone replied. He pointed at a sign nearby, which said: CASSELLI COSTRUZIONE. "And the ownership is right."

"We should call for backup," the young man said.

"There are probably one or two people guarding her," Stone said. "There are four of us, and you have automatic weapons."

"We should let the Naples police handle this."

"Casselli probably owns the Naples police. Call Lugano."

The man produced a phone and pressed a button. "Jim," he said, "we're in Naples with Barrington and Bacchetti. We may have found the building." He listened for a moment. "It fits the description, it's enclosed, and there are lights on at the top floor. Barrington thinks it would be lightly guarded. He wants to go in. What do you want us to do?" He handed the phone to Stone.

"Yes, Jim?"

"This is highly irregular, but it has a good chance of producing results."

"I agree on both counts."

"The Agency can't take responsibility for the girl's life."

"That is my responsibility."

"As long as you understand that."

"I understand it."

"My guys go in first."

"You won't get an argument from me on that."

"Not that you and Dino haven't been through a door or two, but it must have been a while."

"Right on both counts."

"But my guys have the better weapons."

"Dino and I will back them up." He looked at Dino.

Dino nodded. "We'll back them up."

"Call me when it's over, and I'll deal with the local police."

"I'll do that." He handed the phone back to the young man, who listened for instructions, then hung up.

"Whenever you're ready," Stone said.

"Let's pull the cars up to the elevator and point them at the street."

"Good idea."

They moved the cars, and Stone got his spare magazines from the glove compartment and pocketed them; Dino checked his weapon.

The two young men removed two Heckler & Koch machine guns and donned vests. "Any advice?" the young man asked.

"Shoot first and ask questions later," Stone said. "And don't shoot at any females, unless they're pointing weapons at you."

"You have any idea how this elevator works?"

"I expect you press the up button," Stone replied.

The elevator was not locked, and the four men got on, the younger ones first, so they'd be the first out through the door facing the building.

"It's going to make a lot of noise," Dino said, "so they might be ready for us."

The young man pressed the button, and the elevator started up. It was slow, and as Dino had pre-dicted, noisy. They squeaked and rattled their way up the building. Stone reckoned it was twenty-five or thirty stories, but he forgot to count.

Before he had expected it, the elevator came to a sudden stop. The young man held up a hand, then pointed. "We've got some cover," he said. A few steps from the elevator there was a stack of what looked like bags of cement or plaster.

"So have they," Stone said. "Let's go."

The young man opened the door and ran to the stack, sheltering behind it, and was closely followed by his companion, Stone, and Dino.

They stopped and listened. From somewhere be-hind the stack, music was playing.

The young man stood up straight, peered over the stack, and ducked back behind it, shaking his head.

Stone stood up and looked. A dozen feet beyond the stack was another stack.

"Let's get over there," he said.

The two young men led the way to the next stack, then the leader had another look. This time he didn't duck back but walked around the stack and stopped.

His companion followed, and so did Stone and Dino. They were standing on a floor that was empty of anything, except the two stacks of bags.

"Let's check it out," Dino said.

The four men spread out and began searching the floor, while the music got louder. The floor was dimly lit by a dozen hanging lightbulbs scattered around the ceiling. In the middle of the floor were two sawhorses with a plank laid across them. On the plank rested a radio, plugged into one of the wires from the ceiling.

Stone turned it off. "Wrong building," he said.

# 34

It was late when they got back to Marcel's apartment, and Stone went straight to bed without dinner. His glimmer of hope had been dashed in Naples, and the experience had been exhausting. He slept poorly.

He joined Dino and Viv at breakfast.

"You look tired," Viv said.

"Tired and hungry." He ate a large breakfast, had two cups of strong Italian coffee, and felt better. The butler told them that Marcel had gone downstairs to his office for a meeting.

Jim Lugano showed up not long after breakfast. "I thought you'd like to know that our survey of buildings in Naples got the same results you did by driving around. The building you entered was our best hope."

"I think you should do a survey of buildings under construction by Casselli Costruzione," Stone said.

"I've no idea how many there are," Jim replied. "I'd never heard of the company until yesterday."

"That's probably because Casselli isn't building in Rome, for whatever reason. Maybe the Italians can do a computer search on building permits with his company's name on them."

"Good idea," Jim said. "I'll call Dante in a minute and ask him to do that. In the meantime I wanted you to know that I heard from Langley . . ."

"You mean, Lance?"

"From Langley. Your request is getting serious consideration. They seem to be trying to build a national security case, instead of just one of law enforcement. That's not really what we do."

"I understand. I should think that international organized crime would constitute a threat to national security."

"I've made that case to the powers that be," Jim said. "We'll hear from them in due course."

"That sounds like a long wait."

"Not necessarily—we can move quickly."

"I hope you're right."

"In the meantime, we've had a nibble on your offer of a reward for Casselli."

"Oh?"

"Oddly enough, it's from a German citizen who is visiting Rome."

"Does Casselli have business dealings in Germany?"

"It's the European Union—much easier than in the past to do business in different countries."

"Who is he?"

"His name is Frederic Klaucke." Jim spelled it for him. "He's in the chocolate business: an importer."

"Do we have any indication that Casselli has an interest in chocolate?"

"Casselli is interested in money: if chocolate looked profitable, and if he could find a way to make an illegal bundle in it, he'd be interested."

"Okay, what now?"

"Herr Klaucke is in a car downstairs. Shall I ask him up?"

"Let's not invite him into our secure location," Stone said. "Is there somewhere else we could meet him?"

"In one of our vans downstairs in the courtyard?"

"That sounds good. What has he told you so far?"

"Almost nothing. He's had some business dealings with Casselli, that's all he'll say. He wants to speak directly to the person offering the reward."

"Do you think he wants to get at me?"

"No. My sense is, he knows something. It might

not be what we want to know, but it can't hurt to listen to him."

"Tell me what you know about the man."

"He's tall, probably six-two or -three, in his fifties, mostly bald, seems to be well-educated, dresses well."

"Where in Germany is he from?"

"Hamburg. Lives in the suburbs, has offices in the city."

"And he wants to meet me."

"He does. He doesn't know your name, but he's seen the flyer we distributed. Had a copy of it in his pocket, actually."

"This sounds preposterous."

"Maybe it is, who knows? You're the one offering the reward. That would sound preposterous to a lot of people."

"I suppose it would."

"I think the distribution of the leaflet has also told Casselli how much you want Hedy back. I think he looks at five million euros as your opening bid."

"My *opening bid*?"

"Yes."

"He thinks I'm negotiating?"

"Probably. To tell you the truth, I drew the same conclusion."

"Well, you're wrong," Stone said, rising. "Let's go meet with Herr Frederic Klaucke."

# 35

Herr Frederic Klaucke was pacing the courtyard impatiently. His bearing was Prussian, his tan tweed suit so wrinkle-free that it might have been made of cast iron. He was carrying a briefcase that must have belonged to his grandfather.

"Herr Klaucke?" Stone asked, unnecessarily.

Klaucke stopped marching. "*Ja.* Yes."

"I am the person you wish to speak to."

"May I know your name?"

"I'm sorry, you may not."

"My name is Frederic Freiherr von Klaucke," he said. He did not click his heels. "I would like you to know that." His English was perfectly grammatical, his accent distinct. And he had just announced that he was a member of the German nobility.

"Thank you." Stone indicated the open door of the Mercedes van. "Would you like to sit down?"

"Yes, please." He climbed into the van and took a seat; Stone followed him, and Jim Lugano was right behind.

"What have you to tell us?" Stone asked.

"I wish to tell you of Leonardo Casselli."

"Please do."

"I have just spent three days in his company. Involuntarily."

"Are you saying that Mr. Casselli kidnapped you?"

"In the manner of speaking."

"For what purpose?"

"He wished to sell me a great deal of chocolate."

"Are you not a chocolate merchant?"

"No, I am an importer of chocolate, I am not a retailer. I import chocolate, refine it, add other ingredients, like fruit or *nusse*—nuts, that is—and wholesale it to merchants." He opened the briefcase, which Stone assumed had been searched, and extracted a very large chocolate bar containing hazelnuts and handed it to Stone. "Is complimentary, please."

Stone accepted the chocolate bar, which was labeled 500 kg, or half a kilo, or 1.1 pounds. "Thank you."

"Mr. Casselli called me in Hamburg, where I have

my offices, and invited me to come to Rome at his expense to discuss what he described as a very large business deal."

"I am not aware that Mr. Casselli is in the chocolate business."

"Nor am I, especially after our meeting."

"Where did you meet?"

"At a hotel conference room."

"Which hotel?"

"I am not aware of that, either. I was met by a van with painted windows. We drove to the hotel. I was escorted in through a kitchen." Klaucke made that sound like a personal affront.

"I see."

"We sat at a conference table, and Mr. Casselli stated his business."

"Which was?"

"Chocolate. He wished to sell me a very large amount of chocolate—perhaps more than three thousand kilos—at an extremely low price, about half what I am accustomed to paying for the finest chocolate."

"And how did you react to his offer?"

"I was immediately suspicious."

"Suspicious of what?"

"Sir," Klaucke said with a note of reproval in his voice, "this is not, as my Jewish competitors would say, kosher."

"You believed the chocolate to be, ah, illegally obtained?"

"I believed so."

"Why?"

"Because it corresponded to a shipment of chocolate that was stolen from one of my competitors in Rome perhaps a week or ten days ago. I believe the American term is 'hijacked.'"

"I see. And how did you respond to Mr. Casselli's offer?"

"I told him I was not in the market for such an amount."

"And how did he respond?"

"He would not believe me, that I would respond so. He seemed to think I was negotiating."

"He was offended?"

"No, just surprised, I think."

"What happened then?"

"I was escorted back outside, put in a van, and driven to a hotel somewhere outside Rome, where I was imprisoned for three days."

"What sort of hotel?"

"A quite comfortable one, with room service and TV."

"What was its name and location?"

"I was not given that information."

"So you don't know where you were?"

"I do not. It was within an hour's drive of Rome."

"Did you see Mr. Casselli again?"

"Yes. Every day, I was put into the van and driven somewhere, where Mr. Casselli repeated the offer, each time at a lower price."

"And you continued to decline?"

"I did, and Mr. Casselli became very angry on the third day. Finally, I was driven to the airport, where I saw your advertisement. That was early this morning. I phoned and I was told to come here."

"Baron Klaucke, do you understand that the reward is for information leading to the arrest and conviction of Mr. Casselli?"

"Yes."

"And you understand that he must first be apprehended?"

"Of course."

"You have not told me anything that could be used to find Mr. Casselli or to bring him to a court of law."

"How about kidnapping?"

"You have a point," Stone admitted. "But first we must find Mr. Casselli and arrest him, then convict him of kidnapping on your testimony. Then, and only then, would you receive the reward."

"I assure you of my intention to testify against him." Klaucke handed him a business card. "You may reach me here when the time arises. My bank account number is on the reverse of the card. It is where you may wire the funds."

"Thank you. Baron Klaucke, please search your memory: Is there anything else you can tell me that would help us find and arrest Mr. Casselli?"

Klaucke appeared to search his memory. "I don't think so. May I have a lift to the airport?"

"I'll see to that," Lugano said.

They piled out of the van, shook hands, and Klaucke was driven away.

"Chocolate," Stone said.

"Chocolate, indeed," Lugano echoed. "I'll let the police know about the theft. Who knows, it might be helpful."

"I liked Baron Klaucke," Stone said.

"He was all right."

"He's not afraid of Casselli. That's good."

"He probably has no idea who he is."

# 36

S tone went back upstairs and poured himself some coffee from the buffet.

"What was that all about?" Dino asked.

"Chocolate." Stone placed the huge chocolate bar on the table and told him the story.

"Bizarre," Dino said.

"The story?"

"The chocolate. Why would Casselli want three tons of chocolate?"

"Maybe his minions thought the truck was carrying something more readily marketable."

"No doubt."

"Perhaps it would have been more marketable if he had not chosen an honest man to try and sell it to."

"There's a thought," Dino said.

"What thought?"

"Having failed to sell it to the honest baron, maybe he's looking for a less honest customer."

Stone got out his phone. "Jim? Dino had a thought. Having failed to unload the chocolate on the baron, maybe he's looking for another buyer. Perhaps the police would like to know about that. Thank you, Jim." He put away the phone. "Jim will speak to the police."

"There's somewhere I'd like to go," Dino said.

"Where?"

"The emperor Hadrian's villa. It's about an hour from Rome, near Tivoli."

"I'm game," Stone said. He called Jim and asked if they could use the car again. After a brief conversation, he hung up. "The car is ours for the day, but he can't send our bodyguards. They're out, probably looking for chocolate."

"Suits me," Dino said.

"He also recommended a restaurant in Tivoli for lunch. Viv, you want to join us?"

"No, I think I'll go find Mike Freeman and pretend to work."

"As you wish."

\* \* \*

The GPS in the Fiat knew all. They reached the entrance to the villa in an hour. There, they bought tickets and prepared to walk up a long hill. Dino had a better idea: he went back, flashed his badge, and they opened the gates so that they could drive to the villa.

At the top of the hill, at a visitors' center, they saw a large model of the villa, which was now an elegant ruin.

"Not bad, for a weekend place," Dino said. "It would look good in the Hamptons."

They left the visitors' center and walked onto the grounds of the villa, past lakes and baths and a theater. "This place is enormous," Dino said. "I wonder what kind of a staff he needed to keep it running."

"Slaves, I expect."

They toured the grounds for two hours, then got into the car, entered the address of the restaurant into the GPS, and followed the directions back into Tivoli. The GPS proceeded to conduct them through impossibly narrow streets, in a large circle. They found themselves back in the town.

"There's a large parking area over there," Stone said. "Let's park there and take a cab to the restaurant."

They could not find a parking place. Eventually, they drove to the top of a hill near a large arch and found a space where they could abandon the car.

"There," Stone said. "Jim said it was next to a temple." He pointed at the restaurant.

"Unfortunately," Dino said, "there appears to be a deep gorge and a river between us and there."

They went back down the hill to the open plaza; Stone got out his iPhone and went to Google Maps. He pointed at a bridge. "We cross the bridge and take a right. It's not far."

Presently, they found themselves at the door of Restaurant Sibilla, where a small electric cart was parked. Shortly they were seated on a large terrace, covered by a grapevine with a trunk like an oak, with the Temple of Diana nearby.

They had a superb lunch, but went easy on the excellent wine, since they had to drive back. They spent a good two hours there, then Dino had an idea and asked if they could have a ride back to their car. The electric vehicle was brought up, they got aboard, and began to move. Back at the main street, two young men took more than a normal interest in them. As they crossed the bridge, Dino looked back. "Those two guys are chasing us," he said.

Stone looked back, too; Dino was right. "Fortunately, they're not gaining on us."

They were driven to their car, tipped the driver of the cart generously, and drove back down the hill.

On the way back, they passed the two young men walking up the hill. One of them pulled a gun from his jacket as they passed.

"Uh-oh," Dino said. He glanced into his rearview mirror. "They're getting into a car."

# 37

S tone was behind the wheel. "Don't drive
fast," Dino said.

"You want them shooting at us in town?"

"I don't think they'll do that." As it turned out,
Dino was right; they were on the autostrada back to
Rome before the car pulled up next to them and
shots were fired in their direction. Stars appeared on
their armored windows; Dino climbed into the backseat. "I'll bet they don't have an armored car like
ours," he said. "Let's find out." He rolled down the
window a couple of inches and fired two rounds at
the front seat passenger. Their window glass shat-
tered. "I was right," he said.

It soon became clear that their pursuers were
under-equipped in the armor department.

"What are they doing?" Stone asked.

"They've dropped back behind us, and one of them is on a cell phone."

"You think they're calling for reinforcements?"

"I think we should behave as if they are."

Stone checked the rearview mirror and saw the car rapidly approaching in the fast lane. He slammed on the brakes and cut across two lanes to an exit, while the pursuing car was forced to continue down the autostrada.

"Now we're lost," Dino said. The woman in the GPS was demanding that they make a U-turn as soon as possible.

"She'll recalibrate in a minute," he said.

"I think we should follow her advice and get back on the autostrada. The other guys will be getting off at the next exit."

"Good idea," Stone said, slamming on the brakes and executing a U-turn, then gunning it. "I don't know what kind of engine they've got in this car, but it works," he said, accelerating rapidly back onto the autostrada.

"Don't go too fast, we don't want to catch up to them," Dino said. They passed the next exit. "Now go fast, they'll be on surface roads, looking for us."

Stone quickly achieved 180 kph. "It flies," he said. "You want to get back up here?"

"I think I have a better field of fire from back

here. I've only got the one magazine, though. Give me your gun."

Stone handed back his pistol and the spare magazines. They continued unmolested to the end of the autostrada, where they had to stop and insert a credit card for the toll.

"Uh-oh," Dino said, "I think their buddies are laying for us. You've got a car coming up fast, and there's a shotgun sticking out a rear window."

"Let me try something," Stone said, accelerating, but not so fast that they couldn't keep pace. He checked for nearby traffic, then slammed on his brakes and let the other car drift past; then, when they were just a little past him, he turned into them, smashing his left front fender into their right rear. The car spun, smashed into the guardrail, and came to rest athwart the fast lane, pointed in the opposite direction.

"The PIT maneuver," Dino said. "You've been watching *Cops* on TV."

"How'd you guess?"

They managed to make it back to Marcel's compound without incident. Jim Lugano's people made much of their bent fender and bullet-scarred glass.

*     *     *

Upstairs, Stone found the liquor and poured them both a drink. "That was fun," he said, raising his glass.

"It was, at that," Dino said. "It's been a long time since I shot at anybody."

Lugano came into the room. "I hear you've scarred up my car a bit."

"Isn't that what it's for?" Dino asked. "It's not like we went looking for those guys."

"I can't disagree."

"Question," Stone said. "If those guys were tailing us, how come they waited until we were on the way back before they started shooting?"

"What's your point?" Lugano said.

Stone found a pad and paper and wrote something on it, then handed it to Lugano.

*The only time we discussed where we were going was in this room. I also made a phone call from here to book the table at Sibilla.*

Lugano read the note and nodded. "Give me your cell phone," he said, then left the room. He came back ten minutes later. "The room is clean," he said, "but is your cell phone the original or the new one?"

"It's the old one."

"That's how they knew where you were," Jim said. "They waited until you stopped at Hadrian's Villa, then sent somebody to intercept you. By the time they got there, you had already moved to the restaurant, and they picked you up when you left there, right?"

"Right," Stone agreed. "I guess I'd better start using the new SIM card in the new phone."

"Don't throw the old one away," Jim said. "It might come in useful later."

# 38

Hedy swam up through a fog into something like sunlight, coming from the glass-brick window. They had been feeding her well, she thought, but they had also been drugging her. They had taken away her bonds, too. She was free within the room's space of about eight by eight feet. She figured it was a maid's room, but it showed no signs of having been occupied; the paint was fresh, the furniture new. She heard the door open. The woman came into the room and set a tray down on the table next to the bed. *"Mangia,"* she said.

Hedy got her feet over the side of the bed and looked at the tray. Two fried eggs, pancetta, orange juice, coffee. Which one had they been using to drug her? The eggs weren't scrambled, and they looked untampered with. She stuck a finger in the orange juice and tasted it: a slight bitterness. That one. She took it into the bathroom and flushed it down the toilet, then she went back, ate the eggs, bacon, and bread and drank the coffee. The caffeine made a difference.

How long did they take to come back for the tray? Sometimes until they brought lunch. Maybe she had some time. She retrieved the phone from under the mattress and switched it on: three percent left on the battery; it was going to go any minute. She tried calling Stone, but the call wouldn't go through. She hit the text icon: *Running out of juice. Leaving the phone on until it goes. Find me please!* She set the phone on the windowsill for the best chance of getting a signal. She had no idea if he had received the earlier texts. After it sent, she went through and deleted all the texts she had sent and received.

The phone made a weak little noise. She picked it up and looked at it: the battery on-screen turned red, then the screen went dark. It was done.

From outside she began hearing clanging and banging noises. They went on all day, and she finally figured out that they were dismantling the construction elevator. She had been hearing banging and power tools inside the house for what seemed like days. Now all that was silent; all she heard was a vacuum cleaner, maybe two.

At lunch she feigned sleep when they left a ham sandwich and a glass of milk. She ate the sandwich and poured the milk into the toilet and flushed. She put the dead phone back under the mattress; it was useless, but she didn't want them to know she had it.

As daylight waned, the noises from outside stopped. Was the elevator gone, or were they just quitting for the day? The cleaners in the house were quitting, too, and she heard a new, very faint mechanical noise. Had they replaced the construction elevator with a permanent one? She had no way of knowing.

She took her daily shower and rinsed out her thong and bra, then put them back on to dry on her body, under her jeans and sweater.

It was dark when they brought dinner: pasta with plain tomato sauce and a glass of red wine. She ditched the wine and drank water with her dinner.

Stone tried calling Hedy's phone and texting her, but nothing went through. He checked for texts from her but got nothing.

Jim Lugano turned up and took a sheet of paper from his briefcase. It was a map of Italy, and little red dots had been placed on it around Naples and as far south as Salerno. "These are the buildings with Casselli's company's name on the building permits. Two of them have permits for construction elevators: the one you raided in Naples and one at Ravello, a village on top of the mountain above the Amalfi Coast."

"Then it must be the building at Ravello," Stone said. "Let's get down there."

"Hang on," Jim said, raising a hand. "I've already got people on the way, but darkness will hamper them. They'll find the building early tomorrow, and we'll have it photographed."

"Why don't we just raid it, the way we raided the Naples building?"

"First of all, as I've just explained, we don't know exactly where it is, and we won't know until daylight, when the elevator will be visible. Secondly, your raid in Naples was successful because there was nobody there. If they're holding her at the Ravello site, she'll be guarded, and we'll need all the recon we can get before we go in there. Be patient, Stone."

"I'm running out of patience," Stone said. "I'm going to explode soon, if we don't get some leads to follow. Anything on the chocolate?"

Lugano laughed. "Nothing on the chocolate. It's in a truck somewhere, and we have no idea where to look."

"And still no trace of Casselli?"

"He knows we're looking for him. He's hiding, and doing a good job of it. Have you had any messages from Hedy?"

"No, I just checked."

"On the new phone or the old phone?"

"Shit!" Stone yelled, and went to get the old phone. He turned it on, hit the messages icon and read, then he handed the phone to Lugano. "She's all out of battery. Did your guys get a location? She turned on the phone, at least long enough to send that text."

Lugano made a call. "Nothing," he said. "Could be the weak battery or a weak signal, or both." He closed his briefcase. "I'll see you this time tomorrow."

# 39

Leo Casselli sat back in his reclining chair and watched CNN. His lap was full of work papers, and the sound was turned down fairly low, but then he heard his name mentioned. He turned up the volume.

"Let's go to our Rome correspondent, Jeff Palmer, for more on this very interesting story," the young female anchor said. The scene cut to a shot of a middle-aged man standing outside the Colosseum.

"Kalie, Leo Casselli, or Leonardo, as he prefers to be called, made headlines in the United States nearly twenty years ago, when a member of the Mafia family he ran in New York ratted him out to a congressional committee. Before the Justice Department could indict him, Casselli vanished and has not been seen in the United States since that time. He has, however, been seen in fashionable hot spots around Italy and France, schmoozing with the glitterati and having his picture taken with scantily clad young women, usually in restaurants. Casselli maintains that he is a retired businessman, but he is rumored to have a finger in the pies of a dozen Italian industries, and his name appears on many building sites around the country." They cut to a shot of a Casselli Costruzione sign outside some under-construction condos.

"But now, the Italian police department that concentrates on the Mafia—the DIA—has taken a sudden, overt interest in speaking to Signor Casselli, and two multimillionaire businessmen, one an American, the other French, have posted flyers around Rome and Naples, offering a cash reward of five million euros, a new passport, and resettlement to anyone who can produce evidence that will put Casselli in prison, preferably forever."

Casselli smiled and leaned back in his recliner; he was enjoying this.

"Trouble is," the reporter continued, "that suddenly, Leo Casselli has vanished from sight, and the police, in spite of an intensive effort, have been unable to locate him. He has not been seen at his two homes, one in Naples and one on the Amalfi Coast, nor has he been dining at any of his favorite restaurants. He was last seen at lunch in a Paris brasserie that he managed to leave, in spite of the fact that it was surrounded by police. And since that time, two of his ostensibly right-hand men have been murdered, some say because Casselli feared their collecting the big reward.

"The Italian police, in spite of several inquiries on my part, have refused to so much as mention Casselli's name, and it seems that his continued absence from the scene has become something of an embarrassment for them. The Rome and Naples newspapers have become interested, though, and they have begun running daily photographs from their files, in an effort to spread the word that the police would like to have a chat with Leo Casselli. The search continues. We'll get back to you with any news."

Casselli turned the volume back down and returned to the papers in his lap. "What's doing with the fucking chocolate?" he asked a man sitting in a smaller chair next to him.

"Don Leonardo, we continue to try and find a buyer for the stuff."

"Where is it?"

"About fifty meters from here, in a refrigerated trailer."

"And how much is that costing me?"

"Only the gasoline, Don Leonardo; the trailer, we stole and repainted."

"I'm sick of that fucking chocolate," Casselli grumbled. "We're going to end up dumping it into the sea."

"That is a possibility, Don Leonardo."

He waved a hand in the air. "Tell them to get this thing moving."

The man got out of his chair, walked to a wall telephone, and spoke into it. From outside, there came the faint sound of an engine starting, and Casselli's living room began to move. His minion staggered back to his chair.

In Rome, Stone had watched the CNN report, too, and Jim Lugano had come into the room while it was running and had taken a seat.

"Good morning, Stone."

"Good morning, Jim."

"As I explained yesterday, two of Casselli's building projects had permits for construction elevators on-site. One of them you've already visited, in Naples, and the other is in Ravello." He laid a stack of photos on the table. "These are of the Ravello site."

Stone picked them up and leafed through them. "I don't see a construction elevator," he said.

"That's because there isn't one. If you'll look at the aerial shot—the one with the sea far below, in the background, you'll see that the only visible access to the building is on the outskirts of Ravello, a narrow stairway cut out of the rock of the mountain, leading down to a broad deck, at what appears to be the rear of the building."

"What sort of building is it?" Stone asked. "It appears to be cut into the mountainside."

"Honestly, I don't know. The building permit says it's a storage facility, but for the life of me I can't see why anyone would store anything there. The seaward side would have an impressive view, though, so it could be a residence."

"So how would they get construction materials in there? Certainly not down that narrow stairway."

"First, on the construction elevator, which would be removed when an interior elevator is available." Jim produced more photographs. "Then like this," he said. "A large flatbed truck pulls up as close as it can get to the rear of the house, and a crane lifts pallets of boxes or pieces of furniture and sets them down on the rear deck, from where they are taken inside by workmen. It appears that someone or some business is moving into the building now."

"This has got to be the place," Stone said, "by a process of elimination, if nothing else."

"Except we're missing the feature we've been searching for: the outside elevator."

"You said they're moving into the place—maybe they were finished with the elevator. Had to happen sometime."

"I expect you're right."

"Maybe there's a more permanent elevator on the other side."

Jim showed him another photo. "The other side is a sheer rock face, nearly three hundred feet above the coastal highway."

Stone looked at the photo. "This is impossible."

"More like impossibly expensive."

"How's that?"

"The only place they could have an elevator would be *inside* the face of the cliff."

"You mean, a vertical shaft cut out of the rock?"

"It's the only thing I can think of."

"Who could afford to do that?"

"Maybe somebody who owns his own construction company," Jim said.

"Can we get plans for the building?"

"They're on the way."

# 40

After sunset, the articulated truck and trailer bearing Leo Casselli pulled to a stop at a wide place in the Amalfi coastal road. This led to a sort of canyon large enough to hold a couple of dozen cars.

The rear doors were opened and a set of steps set in place, and Casselli walked down them.

"This way, Don Leonardo," his minion said. He led the way toward a tall, recently planted hedge that shielded the entrance to the house from sight.

"Very nice," Casselli said, stroking the hedge like a pet.

"This way, Don Leonardo." The man opened a heavy steel door, then another of smoked glass. A couple of steps, and they were in the new elevator.

"Very good," Casselli said. "I told the architect I wanted it big enough for a grand piano."

"The piano is already in place, Don Leonardo. The house is ninety-nine percent ready for use, should you wish to spend the night."

Casselli pressed the top button, and the elevator rose swiftly.

"First, the lower floor for staff, technical equipment, and kitchens, which are connected to the other floors by a dumbwaiter, then the main-floor living quarters, built to your specifications."

The elevator came to rest on the main floor, and the doors slid open, directly into a very large living room, which was beautifully furnished with soft furniture and good art.

"It is like the architect's drawings," Casselli said. "It is very pleasing to me."

"Would you like to see the bedrooms?"

"Yes."

The man led him up a spiral staircase from room to room; each bedroom had a large en suite bath and a sitting room, as well. "And now the master suite," the man said.

Casselli emerged into a large suite with two bathrooms, two dressing rooms, and a large sitting room with a spectacular view of the sea below. Still more art hung there.

"Your clothes have already been placed in your dressing room, Don Leonardo, as per your instructions."

"Is there a cook present?"

"The house is fully staffed as of this moment."

"Then I will have dinner served here," he said, taking a seat in a reclining chair and switching on a six-foot television screen. "Where is the girl?" Casselli asked.

"In a maid's room, on the lower level, awaiting your pleasure."

"I need no pleasure from her, and I have no wish to see her. I merely want to know she is here. When is Sophia due?"

"She is being driven down from Rome, sir, and should be here within the hour."

"Ah, good. Tell the cook to delay dinner until her arrival, and bring us a bottle of the Masi Amerone, the oldest we have."

"Of course, Don Leonardo. You have only to lift the phone and press the upper-right-hand button to page anyone in the house." He left his master to his news show.

\*　　\*　　\*

Stone leafed through the plans that Jim Lugano had brought; Dante, the policeman, had joined them. "This is spectacular," Stone said. There was a profile elevation showing the elevator shaft, plans of each floor, plus drawings of electrical and plumbing installations. There were renderings of each room, showing furniture placement.

"Look," Stone said, pointing, "he even has a grand piano, and it's a nine-footer, if this scale is correct. I wonder how he got it into the house."

Jim applied a scaled ruler to the plans. "The elevator is three by three meters, big enough for the piano and large artwork, too. You only see elevators like that in museums. And there's a security room on the lower level. He's got cameras everywhere."

"If we want to get in there, we're going to need a power failure," Stone said.

"That won't work—he has a fifty-kilowatt generator on the lower level, enough to power the whole place." Lugano looked at him funny. "Stone, you're not thinking about going in there, are you?"

"I don't see how we're going to get Hedy out, unless we do."

"That would not be a quiet operation," Jim replied. "We'd need fifty people, at least. We've got three stories to deal with, plus that elevator."

Stone pointed to the plans. "There are four staff rooms here, on the lower level. That's where Hedy has got to be."

"Yeah? In which one?"

"I'll have to let you know about that," Stone said.

# 41

A squad of Italian police arrived bright and early at a freight yard connected to Leo Casselli. The commanding officer marched into the office and found two people working there. He handed them a search warrant. "I want the registration and insurance documentation for every vehicle and trailer on this lot," he said to the man in charge, "and be quick about it."

"Do you know who owns this place?" the manager whispered to him.

"Yes, I do," the cop whispered back. "It's Leo Casselli's place."

The man blanched. "I will get into big trouble."

"You're already in big trouble," the cop said. "And if I have to tell you again to get moving, I'll put you in handcuffs and tear this place apart."

The man got moving. He went to a filing cabinet and removed a stack of folders. "Here," he said. "This is the file on every piece of equipment in the yard. The serial number for each is written on the outside of the folder."

The cops went to work. Two hours later, the lead cop called his men together. "Have you finished?"

"Yes, sir," one of them said. "Except for that trailer, the refrigerated one—there is no record of it."

"Get me the bolt cutters," he said.

He walked over to the trailer and cut the padlock. "Open it!"

Two men swung open the doors; the trailer was filled to the ceiling with cardboard boxes.

"What is it?" the cop asked.

A man pulled down a box and cut it open. "Candy," he said.

"Bring me those two people from the office."

The two workers were marched out.

"Where is the paperwork for this trailer?"

"Um, there is no paperwork," one of them said. "We arrived for work a couple of days ago, and it was sitting here. We have to refill the tank for the refrigeration unit every day."

"You are both under arrest for the receiving of stolen goods," the cop said, "and every vehicle and trailer on this lot is now confiscated. Bring me the keys for all of them."

"Confiscated?" the man said. "I will be shot."

"It is now all the property of the Italian government," the cop said, "and so are you."

S tone, Dino, and Viv were at lunch, with Jim and Dante as their guests, when Dante's phone rang. *"Pronto."* He listened for a moment. *"Eccellente."* He hung up. "You will all be delighted to know that we have found the missing shipment of chocolate, and that the trailer is parked on a lot owned by Leo Casselli. We have confiscated half a dozen trucks and two dozen trailers and arrested the workers there. It will be interesting to see who makes bail for them."

"Baron Klaucke will be thrilled," Stone said, "but only if this leads to Casselli's arrest and conviction."

"Now we have two provable charges against Casselli," Dante said. "The kidnapping of the baron and the larceny of the chocolate and its trailer. That's progress."

\*       \*       \*

Casselli was having a light lunch when his phone rang. *"Pronto."*

"Don Leonardo," a voice said, "the police have raided your lot in Naples and have discovered the load of chocolate."

Casselli laughed. "They are welcome to it," he said.

"It is worse," the voice said. "They have arrested your two employees on the lot and they have confiscated every vehicle there."

"Confiscated?" Casselli asked, disbelieving. "Call our captain of police in Naples and have this order canceled at once."

"I have already called him," the man said, "and he hung up on me."

"Hung up on you? I don't believe it!"

"He must believe his telephone is tapped."

"What phone are you calling from?"

"My cell phone, Don Leonardo."

"Bail those people out of jail before they start talking!" He hung up.

"Something wrong, darling?" the lovely Sophia asked.

"You might say that," Casselli said, and he was sweating.

*   *   *

Casselli isn't going to like this," Lugano said, smiling.

"Wait until he tries to get his people out of jail," Dante said. "We have moved them south, to Salerno. He is not going to like that a lot!"

"It's about time he started to get nervous," Jim said. "He's not accustomed to being nervous, and when people are nervous, they make mistakes."

# 42

L eo Casselli got back into his truck and was driven to Naples, to a prearranged meeting site. His two top *capos*, newly appointed to fill the places of their departed predecessors, stood before him, looking anguished.

"What is going on here?" Casselli demanded.

"We don't know, Don Leonardo," the braver of the two replied. "Our vehicles are being stopped and ticketed for speeding and broken taillights, even when they were not speeding and their taillights were not broken. Three restaurants have been inspected and closed by the health authorities. Four building sites have been shut down for safety violations. We have security camera footage of four men who entered another site with guns drawn, and all the vehicles at the trucking yard have been confiscated and taken away and two employees arrested. We cannot bail them out, because we can't find them."

"Wait a minute. You said security camera footage?"

"Yes, Don Leonardo. Would you like to see it?"

"Immediately."

The man took a cassette from his briefcase and inserted it into a player, then pressed a button.

Casselli watched intently as the four men entered the top floor of the building and moved around two stacks of building materials. Then they moved toward the radio and came into the light. "Stop it right there!" Casselli said. "Rewind a few seconds. Stop!" He peered at the images. "Do you know these men?"

"Two of them are agents of the DIA, the ones on either end. We don't know the other two."

"I know one of them!" Casselli spat. "His name is Barrington, and he is the partner of Marcel duBois! I want him found and brought to me immediately!"

"Ah, so that is Barrington," the man said. "We know where he is."

"Where?"

"At the building belonging to Marcel duBois. It is surrounded by the police and the DIA, and there are vehicles there registered to the American Embassy."

"Then bring him to me!"

"Don Leonardo, I am sorry to say that the security in the building and its courtyard has been impenetrable for us, and they have discovered and disconnected our cameras and listening devices in the building. On the one occasion that Barrington and his friend left the building and drove to Tivoli, they did so in an embassy vehicle that had bulletproof glass and bodywork, and our attempt to kidnap them failed."

"So now I have to deal not only with the police and the DIA, but the health department, building inspectors, and the Americans?"

"It would appear so, Don Leonardo. I regret that, in the present circumstances, we are unable to carry out your orders."

Casselli glared at the man and waited for him to wilt, but he did not. He began to admire his courage, and, being a practical man, he recognized that what he was being told was true. "Still," he said, "we have an edge."

"We do, Don Leonardo? What is that?"

"Give me a secure cell phone," Casselli said.

The man removed a phone from his pocket and handed it to him.

Casselli looked closely at it. "This cannot be traced?"

"We change them every day," the man said. "That one has not yet been used."

Casselli took a notebook from his pocket and found a number, then dialed it.

S tone was alone in the living room when his phone rang. He checked caller ID and saw nothing. "Hello?"

"Good day, Mr. Barrington," Casselli said. "Do you know who this is?"

Of course he knew, but he wanted Casselli to say it. "No. Who are you?"

"This is Leonardo Casselli."

"Oh, yes, I remember you. I last saw you running from a Paris restaurant, ahead of the police."

"Very far ahead. It was duplicitous of you to try to take me, and worse, ineffective."

"What can I do for you, Leo?" He knew Casselli hated being called that.

"How would you like to buy back the girl?"

"I would have to speak to her, before I can even discuss that," Stone said. "I will need proof of life. Surely you have kidnapped people before—you know how these things are done."

"I can arrange for you to hear her scream," Casselli said through clenched teeth.

"Come now, Leo, making threats will not get us

to a mutually satisfying conclusion. What do you want?"

"Fifty million euros," Casselli said, "and the attention of the police withdrawn."

Stone laughed aloud and hung up the phone. He called Lugano.

"Yes?"

"Casselli just called. Did you get a trace on him?"

"On which phone?"

"The old one."

"No. Our system can only do two searches at a time. Capacity is taken up by a watch on your new cell and Hedy's phone."

"Shit. Hedy's phone is dead. Take it down and concentrate on my two phones."

"All right. What did Casselli have to say?"

"He's feeling the heat," Stone said. "He wanted fifty million euros and, get this, the police and the DIA off his back."

"Jesus, is he serious about the money?"

"Of course not, he's just trying to show me he has the upper hand. He wouldn't let me speak to Hedy. That indicates to me that he and she are not in the same place. He threatened to torture her."

"What did you say to him?"

"I hung up the phone."

"Well, that was gutsy of you."

"What else could I do? I'm not going to give him fifty million euros, even if I could raise it."

"Well then, I suppose the next move is his. Let's see what he comes up with."

"Right." Stone hung up, hoping that Casselli's next move was not Hedy screaming into the phone.

# 43

Casselli sat, fuming. The insolence of this Barrington! He was unaccustomed to being
spoken to in that manner, and no one, but
no one, ever got away with hanging up on him during
a telephone conversation. He turned to the two men.
"I have a rather distasteful job for you," he said.

"Anything, Don Leonardo," they said in unison.

"I need you to go and take the finger of a young
woman." He explained exactly how he wanted it done.

"Which finger, Don Leonardo?" one of them
asked.

"Oh, let's see, how about right index?"

"It shall be done, Don Leonardo."

\*    \*    \*

S tone and Dino were having a drink with Viv and Marcel at the end of the day, when a package was delivered.

"Who is this from?" Stone asked.

"We don't know, but it's not explosive. It's an object about three inches long," the DIA agent said. "Would you like me to open it?"

"Please," Stone said.

The young man produced a switchblade, flicked it open, and cut the tape around the box. He removed the lid and handed it to Stone.

Whatever it was was in an envelope of suede leather, like something from a jewelry store. Stone opened it and shook out the contents into the box. He blanched. The object was a human finger, with a brightly painted nail. "Jesus Christ."

Jim Lugano came into the room. "I heard there was a package delivered," he said. "Was it checked out?"

Stone handed him the box. "I checked it out, and I'm sorry I did."

"Well," Lugano said, looking at the thing, "that's gory. Do you recognize it as being Hedy's?"

"I've no idea. I never examined her fingers."

Jim pointed at the young Italian agent. "You. Come with me." The two men left the room. Twenty minutes later, Jim returned. "I've sent it to the police lab. Do you know if Hedy has ever been finger-printed?"

Stone shook his head.

"Military service? Arrest? Application for a gun license? Anything?"

"I don't know," Stone said. "Run the print and see what you come up with."

"That's being done," Jim said. "I'm going to go over to the lab and see what they're finding out. Do you want to come?"

"No, thanks," Stone said. "Right now I'm working on not losing my lunch."

"I'll call you when I know something."

"Try for some more cheerful news," Stone said. Jim left, and the others sat there, silent. "Maybe I shouldn't have hung up on Casselli," Stone said at last.

"Stone, this is not your fault," Viv said.

"Isn't it? The worst luck Hedy has ever had was meeting me on an airplane. This wouldn't have happened to her otherwise."

They sat, mostly in silence, for another hour or so; then Stone's phone rang, and he got it out of his pocket.

"Just a moment," Viv said. She took a small object from her pocket and affixed it to the back of his phone. "Now answer it."

Stone pressed the button. "Hello?"

"You don't sound so good," Casselli said. "Has something upset you?"

Stone was silent.

"It was very quick, you understand, and a nurse was standing by, so no permanent damage has been done." He paused for a beat. "Yet."

Stone still couldn't speak.

"Of course, it was very painful—nothing to be done about that."

"You miserable piece of shit," Stone was finally able to say. "I hope I find you before the police do."

"That would be a very interesting meeting," Casselli replied. "Now, are you ready to negotiate the release of the girl?"

"I won't negotiate with you."

"I don't know what it takes to move you, Mr. Barrington. Shall I send you more body parts? Would you like to return them to her parents?"

Stone hung up. Viv took the phone from him, tapped some keys, and replayed the conversation. Everyone listened, rapt. "Good man," Viv said when it was done.

Jim Lugano strode into the room. "Relax," he said, "the finger doesn't belong to Hedy."

"How do you know?" Stone asked.

"We found her prints from an application she

made for a Global Entry pass, the thing that gets you through airport security in a hurry. No match. Also, the lab says the finger, though recently severed, had been refrigerated for several days. The finger was probably taken at a morgue. Finally, we got a hit on the print from the Italian database: the woman it belonged to had an arrest record for prostitution in Naples."

Stone heaved a loud sigh. "When you find Casselli, I hope you'll give me a few minutes alone with him."

# 44

Casselli paced back and forth across his new living room. He had been faced with unco-operative victims before, but never one like Barrington. Normally, he could beat, shoot, or bomb a holdout into submission, but Barrington, in addition to being a hardhead, had the connections to make himself unavailable for mayhem or murder.

Finally, Casselli turned to a minion. "Bring the girl to me," he said.

Moments later, Hedy was marched into the living room. "Ah, Miss Kiesler," Casselli said. "I won't detain you long." He held up a finger, then pressed the redial button on his phone.

\*　　\*　　\*

S tone answered the call on speaker, so everyone in the room could hear the conversation. "Yes?"

"You said you wished to speak to the girl," Casselli said.

Before Stone could reply, he heard Hedy's voice, shouting, "Wow, what a view! I can see almost as far as Capri!"

There were sounds of a scuffle.

"Did you hear that?" Casselli asked.

"Hear what?"

"The voice of your lover."

"All I hear is you."

"You still wish to speak with her?"

"Certainly."

Hedy came on. "Don't do what he wants, Stone!" she shouted. "If he hurts me, Arthur will destroy him!"

There were more sounds of struggle, then Casselli came back on. "There, did you hear that?"

"Yes, and I will follow her instructions to the letter," Stone said. "You don't know what you've gotten yourself into, Leo. She's right about Arthur—he will destroy you." Stone hung up.

"Who the hell is Arthur?" someone asked.

"Hedy's stepfather, Arthur Steele."

"Who is he?"

"He's an insurance executive."

"Does he have the means to destroy Casselli?"

"No, but Casselli doesn't know that."

Everyone burst out laughing.

Kill her!" Casselli screamed at his men. "Cut her into pieces, and send them to Barrington!"

"Yes, Don Leonardo," one of them said, and the men began to drag her from the room.

"Wait a minute!" Hedy yelled.

Astonished, they stopped.

"What?" Casselli shouted.

"I want a priest."

"Are you insane?" Casselli asked.

"I'm a good Catholic, I want to make my confession and have the last rites of the Church!"

"I'm not going to get you a priest!"

"Are you a Catholic?"

"Of course!"

"Then you can't deny me a priest!" Hedy was not a Catholic, and she had no idea whether this was correct. "You will go directly to hell, no purgatory!"

Casselli stopped talking; his jaw worked, but no sound came out.

"And if you murder me, I will prepare the way for you to hell's gates!" She groped for something else to say. "And Arthur is a friend of the Pope! He will ask him to excommunicate you immediately!" This was a bald-faced lie; Arthur was Jewish, and he had no acquaintances in the Vatican that she knew of.

"You are worse than this Barrington!" Casselli shouted. He waved a hand. "Take her back to her room!"

"Do you still want us to kill her, Don Leonardo?" one of the men asked.

"No. Not yet! When I say!"

The men dragged Hedy away. "You don't know who you're dealing with!" she shouted back at him.

Casselli sank into a chair and mopped his brow. Perhaps she was right; maybe he didn't know who he was dealing with.

First, this Barrington, now this Arthur, who was a friend of the Pope! Casselli didn't even know the Pope! He wasn't much of a Catholic, but he feared the Church. If he killed this girl, she would precede him into the next world, and the Church's wrath would be waiting for him.

S he's confirmed her location," Stone said. "She said she could almost see Capri."

"Dante," Jim Lugano said, "do we have enough on Casselli to raid this house on the cliff?"

"Having enough is not the problem," Dante replied. "It would require nothing less than a full-scale military assault to take the place, and the girl could die in the middle of that. We would be moving out of the world of criminal justice and into the world of politics, where anything could happen. Who knows who Casselli has bought?"

"We're just going to have to find another way," Stone said.

# 45

Hedy was returned to her little room and locked in. But in the past minutes—the first time she had been let out of her prison—she had learned a few things. They were on the Amalfi Coast, she had been right about that. Now she had to start finding a way out of this room and then out of the house.

She found a wire coat hanger in her closet and began trying to shape part of it into a lock pick. She didn't know much about picking locks, but this one was large and old-fashioned and used a large key. She worked on it until dinner came, and at the scraping of the key in the lock she jumped back onto the bed.

Lasagna this time; she ate it greedily, pouring the wine down the toilet, as usual. Maybe picking the lock had not been such a good idea. The woman who brought the food was a little smaller than she; maybe she could be overcome. She knew where the key was—in her apron pocket. She looked around for a weapon, should she need it. Nothing, only a rickety caned chair, very old. Nothing to tie the woman up with, either, and she would have to be gagged, too, and there was nothing for that, unless she started tearing up the sheets. She tried it, but without a cutting tool, she couldn't make it work.

She thought of bribing the woman, but she didn't have any money to show her, and she was unlikely to accept a promise of funds later. She would also be afraid of her employer.

Hedy went back to working on the coat hanger.

A couple of hours later, she began experimenting with the pick she had made. She had bent one end to a right angle by clamping it in a drawer and bending the long end. Then she made another, larger right angle at the other end to use as turning leverage. The whole thing was, maybe, four inches long. She was surprised once, when she heard the key scrape in the lock and barely had time to duck into the bathroom and flush the toilet before the woman came in and took her tray. When Hedy came out she was alone again and went back to work on the key. Finally, she got it placed inside the lock and thought she had found a sweet spot. Using both hands, she turned the other, larger end and felt something inside move. A moment later the door was unlocked.

She cracked it open and listened. There was conversation in Italian from the kitchen between two women, who from the sound of their activity were cleaning up. She closed the door softly. She would wait until later, when the house was asleep.

It was well past midnight, she thought, when she opened the door and listened again. No voices, no pots clattering, just silence. She was in a hallway, and there were other doors like her own, numbered. She was in three. The household workers must be asleep in one, two, and four. No light shined from under the doors. She took off her shoes and, holding them in one hand, moved slowly and silently down the hall, emerging into a kitchen, large and commercial-looking. There she found a door that seemed to lead farther to the rear of the house. On her way she spotted a waiter's corkscrew and stuffed it into her jeans pocket with the lock pick; she wasn't sure why, but it had a blade that might come in handy. It occurred to her later that she could have found a proper knife in the kitchen.

She opened the door, which led into another hallway and several storage rooms. She could see another door at the end, and she made her way to it. Locked. The top half was of glass panes, and she could see trees moving in the darkness and hear the wind blowing. She inspected the lock with her fingers. There was no thumbscrew; it must be locked with a key.

She felt the ledge above the door: nothing. She ran her fingers along the inside wall, and found it: a teacup hook, with a key dangling from it. She felt her way back to the lock, slipped the key into it, and turned. It opened. She removed the key and let herself out, locking it behind her. It would stop anyone chasing her, until they could find another key.

She leaned against the door for a moment to let her heart slow its beating and her eyes become accustomed to the darkness. She fought the exhilaration that came with being free; she still had to be careful. She stood on the edge of a broad deck and saw an opening in the handrail ahead. She crossed the expanse quickly and stopped at the opening. There was a path, and it led upward.

Then she heard a terrible sound: someone was trying to open the door behind her, and in a moment they would know the key was gone. Rain began to fall. She moved ahead quickly, feeling her way. The path began to narrow as she climbed. Then the clouds broke for a moment, long enough to let some moonlight through. She saw that the right side of the path was a sheer drop into a void, and there was only a rope handrail between her and that void.

The moon vanished again, leaving her in pitch darkness, with only her memory of the scene to guide her.

She plunged ahead into the black night, doing her best to stay to her left. Then she fell, stretching her arms out, trying to catch the rope. Instead, she caught a blow to the head.

# 46

Everyone seemed happier at dinner. They knew that Hedy was alive and well, and they knew where she was. As for rescuing her, nobody seemed to have a clue, short of a commando assault, and nobody wanted that.

"How about a drone?" Stone asked. He had had a recent experience with drones that had frightened him with their capabilities.

"We have access to drones," Lugano said.

"So have we," Dante echoed.

"What would you do with a drone?" Lugano asked.

"I don't know: spy on him? Get a closer look at the house? Maybe figure out where they're holding her?"

"We've got detailed plans of the house," Lugano

pointed out, "and as for where they're holding her, my money's on one of the maids' rooms. From what we heard on the phone call, I don't think Hedy's bunking in with Casselli."

"If we could get Hedy out first," Stone said, "I wouldn't mind firing a Hellfire missile into the place. In fact, I'd be glad to pull the trigger."

"Overkill," Dante said. "We wouldn't have anyone left to try, and I very much want a trial."

A servant brought an envelope to Lugano. "This just came by messenger," he said. "It's addressed to you and Mr. Barrington."

Lugano opened it and found another envelope inside, along with a letter on handsome stationery with a crest at the top. "It's from Baron Klaucke," he said. He read from the letter. "'This arrived today. It may have been intended ironically. Please add it to the evidence I am providing.'" Lugano opened the other envelope and extracted an invitation. He read it slowly. "It doesn't say who it's from, but there's an ornate *C* at the top." He read: "'The pleasure of your company is requested for a housewarming. Drinks, dinner, and music.' There's an address on the Amalfi Coast road."

"When?"

"Saturday, in three days, drinks at seven."

"Why would Casselli invite Klaucke to his party?"

"Because he's a baron? Maybe Casselli is a snob."

"I think we should accept on Baron Klaucke's behalf," Stone said, "but without an RSVP."

They moved to the living room for coffee and brandy.

"We can't attack," Jim said, "but Stone's right, we can infiltrate."

"Disguised as guests?" Stone asked. "I don't think we could pass for Casselli's friends."

"But," Jim pointed out, "there will be a lot of other people in the house—staff, catering personnel, musicians."

Dante brightened. "On another occasion we smuggled our people into a large event as workers. It could work again."

"How would you manage it?" Stone asked.

"The same way we did before: we find out who's catering the affair and what sort of music is being provided. We substitute our people for some of theirs."

"I play bass," Lugano said, raising his hand. "Most Sunday nights at a jazz club."

"One of my assistants plays very good jazz guitar," Dante said, "in the manner of Django Reinhardt. All we need is a pianist who knows how to use a gun."

"Stone is likely to shoot himself in the foot," Dino said, "but he plays pretty decent piano."

"Oh, no," Stone said, "I'm the rustiest piano player you ever heard."

"Let's hear something," Lugano said, taking away Stone's drink and pointing him at the piano in the corner.

"Casselli's file says he's a music lover," Dante said, "with a particular fondness for the Great American Songbook."

"All right," Stone said, "I'll play you some Rodgers and Hart, but it will sound a lot better if you're all talking at the same time." He sat down and played "My Romance," and got a round of hearty applause from the group.

"You'll do," Jim said. "Where have you played?"

"I picked up spending money when I was at NYU, at a little club on Bleecker Street called the Surf Maid."

"I've been in there," Jim said. "A nine-foot grand with stools around it and a bar."

"That's the joint. I warn you, I don't have the chops anymore for up-tempo stuff."

"Okay, we'll keep it sedate."

"So we have ourselves a trio," Dante said, taking out his phone. "I'll get on the search for what agency is supplying the music and what caterer has the job, then we'll start threatening them." He walked to one side of the room and began speaking Italian into the phone.

"Problem," Stone said. "Casselli knows me—we had lunch, remember?"

"Don't worry," Jim said, "one of the great skills harbored in our Agency is that we are masters of disguise. We have a guy who can turn you into Ray Charles."

"I don't do blackface," Stone said.

"You could do George Shearing," Viv contributed.

"I don't look anything like Shearing."

"Just the dark glasses. You can play blind—you just never look directly at anybody. If you're talking to someone, you look over his shoulder somewhere. But you can't look at your hands when you play."

"Dark glasses and a mustache might do it," Jim said. "Maybe a better nose."

"What's wrong with my nose?" Stone asked.

"It's too good," Viv said. "Jim's right. His make-up man could mess it up a little, give your face character."

"Casselli will never make you," Jim said. "I promise."

# 47

Hedy was stunned for a moment but quickly recovered. She could hear footsteps on the wooden deck behind the house. An outside light came on.

Hedy got to her feet and climbed over a rock to her left. She cowered in a crevice as footsteps went past her on the path, then they retreated back to the deck.

"Nobody out here," a man said in Italian. "Where did the key go?" He went inside, and she heard the door lock behind him.

Hedy discovered a niche under her rock and crawled into it. She was dry, if not warm, and she was in no mood to go blindly along that path in the rain. Soon she was asleep.

When she woke the rain had stopped, and the sun

shone intermittently, enough to warm the air comfortably. She was hungry, but she wasn't ready to risk the trail in daylight. She'd wait until dark, and if it wasn't raining, try it again. She crawled out of her shelter and looked around. A few feet away was the rope handrail on the path, which led along a sheer cliff face and seemed to narrow to almost nothing. In the other direction was a lovely view of the sea and mountains and, a few feet away, what seemed another sheer drop-off. She was trapped on a peninsula of stone, with the path leading to the house, and in the other direction, God knew what awaited her.

Then she heard something odd: the sound of hooves on stone. She peered over a rock and saw an old man picking his way along the path on the cliff face, leading a donkey, which was heavily laden. As he passed slowly toward the house she saw that the donkey was carrying groceries, and she managed to swipe two apples and a banana before he had passed her. She retreated to her hiding place and had the banana for breakfast. The apples would have to do for breakfast and lunch.

Then she heard a woman's voice shrieking, "Gone! The girl is gone!" People in the house rushed about talking loudly, then it got quiet again.

*   *   *

Casselli sat in the living room, going over a list. "I make it fifty-eight, with wives and girlfriends," he said to his secretary.

"Only the man Klaucke, from Germany, did not respond," she said. "Everyone else accepted."

"We have the caterer from Rome, correct?"

"Yes, Don Leonardo. And the musicians, a quartet of jazz."

"Good."

A man entered the room carefully. "Don Leonardo," he said, "there has been an incident."

"What sort of incident?"

"The girl is gone."

"Gone? Gone where?"

"No one knows, Don Leonardo. When she was taken her breakfast, she wasn't there. The door was locked, as usual," he lied.

"Have you searched the house?"

"Yes, Don Leonardo, every room, closet, and corner. She is not here."

"How could she get out of the house?"

"The only irregularity we have discovered is that the key to the rear door to the deck is missing. It was hanging on a hook in the hallway. But we have a spare key."

"You think she got out the rear door?"

"It's possible, Don Leonardo. I myself have

walked the path to the village both ways, and she is nowhere to be found. It's possible that she may have slipped on the path in the dark and fallen into the ravine, but we cannot see a body anywhere."

"Take the elevator down and search the parking area. She would have fallen there, likely."

"Yes, Don Leonardo," and he beat a retreat.

Strangely, Casselli felt relieved that the girl was out of his house. He hadn't known what to do with her.

The man was back in fifteen minutes. "There is no sign of the girl anywhere near the road."

"Could she have climbed down the rock face to the parking area?"

"In the dark? Impossible, I think. I believe she must have got to the village or beyond, though I would not wish to attempt the path in the night, without an electric torch."

"She could go to the police, but they would call here, wouldn't they?"

"Of course, Don Leonardo. They are in your pocket. Do you have further instructions for me?"

"No, no, get out."

"It is a good thing," his secretary said. "The girl was a pain in the ass. I hope she fell down the ravine and broke her neck."

"From your lips to God's ear."

"The flowers and extra liquor have been ordered and will be delivered in due course," the woman said. "The tableware and glasses are being delivered today. It's going to be a wonderful party."

"Yes," he said, "wonderful. I'm looking forward to seeing everybody. I've been cooped up for too long."

Hedy passed the afternoon napping. She tried her cell phone again, but it was truly dead. When it got dark, she would go back into the house for some food. Maybe she would find a flashlight, too; she could make it along the path in the dark with a flashlight.

# 48

Stone called Arthur Steele, in New York.

"Have you news, Stone?"

"Good news," Stone replied. "Hedy is alive and well, and we have a location for her."

"Why haven't you retrieved her?"

"She is in a house built into a cliff face on the Amalfi Coast," Stone said. "The only way to take it immediately would be by a military attack, and that would be very dangerous for Hedy. The police have elected to infiltrate instead. On Saturday night the owner is throwing a housewarming. The police are placing people on the catering staff and as musicians and will take it from inside, after having secured Hedy."

"God, I'm glad I haven't told her mother about this," Arthur said.

"I think you were right not to. Casselli has made a

halfhearted attempt to extort money in exchange for Hedy."

"How much is he asking?"

"Fifty million euros. That's how we know he's not serious."

"You were right not to agree to that, Stone."

"If you can hang on until Sunday, I think we'll have good news."

"I'll do my best." The two men hung up.

"How are Arthur and his wife holding up?" Dino asked.

"Arthur hasn't told his wife, so she's just fine. Arthur is well-named—he's a steely guy."

Jim and Dante got off the elevator.

"Any progress?" Stone asked.

"We've located the businesses that are supplying the catering and music, and my people are working on them now," Dante said. "We should have everything wrapped up this morning, with any luck at all."

"Have these people dealt with Casselli before?"

"They've dealt with his secretary, who is making the arrangements."

"Do they know that if we're successful Saturday night, they'll lose a customer?"

"I've authorized my people to offer very attractive financial incentives—the minister has approved the money."

Dante's phone rang, and he stepped aside to answer it. Shortly, he returned. "A small problem," he said. "The jazz group that was being furnished for Casselli's party has agreed to a buyout for the evening."

"Then what's the problem?" Stone asked.

"Casselli is expecting a quartet. We need a drummer."

"So, hire a drummer."

"We can't take a civilian musician in there. Anyway, the agent says nobody's available on short notice. I don't want you to show up there with a smaller group than has been paid for."

"So what do we do?" Stone asked.

"We're all out of ideas."

"Relax," Dino said, "I play drums."

Stone stared at him. "That's a joke, right?"

"It is not."

"You just want to go along on this raid. You'll embarrass us with your ham-handed efforts."

"How well do you play?" Jim asked.

"About as well as Stone plays piano," Dino replied. "I played in the high school band and the dance band, too. Oh, and I'm not a civilian like Stone, and I'm good with being armed."

"Stone? Shall we take a chance on Dino's drumming?"

"I want him to audition," Stone said.

"Oh, come on!" Dino yelled.

"I had to audition, I want Dino to audition, too. I think his high school story is fishy—he's never said anything to me about playing drums."

"Okay," Dino said, "get me some drums."

"I play with a drummer on Saturday nights," Jim said," but he'll be using his drums."

"Ask him where we can rent or buy a set in Rome," Dino said.

Jim made the call, then hung up. "There's a place called Drum City, out in the burbs to the south."

"Let's go, then," Dino said.

"Dante, are drums in the budget?"

"I'm not sure how to explain that to the minister."

"What the hell," Dino said, "I'll buy them and take them home with me."

"No, you will not!" Viv said. "I'm not living with a drummer!"

"I'll find the money," Dante said.

Two hours later, Dino was all set up in Marcel's living room, next to the piano. He sat down behind the set and played a roll, followed by a cymbal crash. "Okay," he said, "let's do it."

"How much did he make you spend?" Stone asked Dante.

Dante winced. "Twelve hundred euros, and change. Dino insisted on the best stuff—said his reputation was at stake."

"God," Viv said, "I'm glad you're not taking them home."

# 49

Arthur Steele put the phone down and buzzed his secretary.

"Yes, Mr. Steele?"

"Get me Cardinal Prizzi at the Vatican."

"Yes, sir." She came back after a minute. "The cardinal is on the line."

"Arturo! How are you?"

"Not as good as I should be, Pietro."

"I'm so sorry to hear that. How can I be of help?"

"I'm very sorry to have to come to you with this, Pietro."

"Nonsense! Anything, *anything* I can do. You have only to ask."

"My wife's daughter has been kidnapped in Italy."

"I am astonished! How has this happened?"

"A mafioso named Casselli has taken her and demanded a ransom."

"*Leo* Casselli? That one?"

"That one."

"But how do you come to be in business with this man?"

"I am not in business with him. I have had nothing to do with him. A friend and associate of mine met Hedy in Rome. Perhaps you know Marcel du-Bois?"

"You are doing business with Marcel?"

"No, with Marcel's partner, a very fine man named Stone Barrington."

"Spell."

Arthur spelled.

"He and Marcel are building a hotel in Rome, and Casselli is trying to extort money from them, promising to pave their way. They need no help in that regard."

"Shocking!"

"Hedy is being held at a property belonging to Casselli on the Amalfi Coast. Casselli is demanding a ransom of fifty million euros."

"No! You must not pay it, Arturo, this will not guarantee the return of your daughter. Have you spoken with the police?"

"Yes, and they are trying very hard to help, but

they are afraid to go in there for fear that Hedy will be killed in the assault."

"Infamous! How can I help?"

"I confess I don't know, Pietro. I have no ideas. My wife will take her own life if anything happens to her daughter. I am distraught."

"Arturo, I will call you back in an hour."

"All right."

The cardinal buzzed his secretary, and the young priest entered his office. "Yes, Your Eminence?"

"That invitation I told you to decline—do you still have it?"

"I made the call—I think it must still be in my wastebasket."

"Find it."

The priest left and returned after a moment. The cardinal stared at it. "Call this number and get Leonardo Casselli on the phone immediately." He sat, tapping his finger, for perhaps a minute.

Mr. Casselli, Cardinal Prizzi of the Vatican Bank is on the line."

"You're shitting me!"

"I am not. Will you speak to him?"

"Of course I will speak to him, you stupid bitch!" Casselli shouted, snatching the phone from her. "Yes, Your Eminence?"

"Hold for the cardinal," the priest said.

Leo Casselli was not a religious man, but he was a superstitious one. He feared the Church as a teenager might fear zombies. He was instantly terrified.

The phone buzzed, and the cardinal picked it up. "Yes?"

"Casselli on line one."

Prizzi picked up the phone. "Casselli?"

"Yes, Your Eminence," Casselli oozed. "What an honor to hear from you personally!"

"What do you know of honor, you pig?"

Casselli made a gulping noise. "I'm sorry, Your Eminence? Have I somehow . . . inadvertently . . . offended you?"

"You offend the human race by belonging to it," the cardinal spat. "I will damn you to hell!"

"Oh, Your Eminence," Casselli said, his bowels turning to water, "how have I offended you?"

"You have kidnapped the daughter of my friend Arturo!"

Casselli remembered the name. Could the girl not have been lying? "Oh, Your Eminence, I would never do such a thing, I swear to you. The girl was a guest in my home—it was all very proper."

"Was? Have you harmed the girl?"

"Oh, no, Your Eminence! I would never harm her. She is such a sweet girl."

"Let me speak to her."

Casselli gulped again. "I am so sorry, she is not here. She left my house late last night, of her own free will!" At least that was not a lie, he thought.

"Where is she?"

"I think she might have returned to Rome."

"If you kidnapped her, she would not have a car."

"Ah, um . . . perhaps she hitchhiked?"

"You find that girl, and you return her to her father at once!"

"But, Your Eminence, I have no idea where she is."

"You have harmed her, haven't you? Hedy would not leave there in the middle of the night in that awful storm we had. What have you done with her?"

"If you wish, Your Eminence, I will send my people out to find her."

"You had better do that, and fast. If you have not

found the girl by tomorrow, your soul will be in mortal danger. Call my office!" The cardinal slammed down the phone.

Casselli was astonished to find that he had peed in his pants.

# 50

rthur Steele's phone rang at home. "Hello?"

"Arturo, it is Pietro."

"Pietro, thank you for calling."

"I have good news: your daughter is alive and, presumably, well."

"Thank God."

"I spoke to this swine Casselli myself, and he assured me that she left his house last night."

"Where is she now?"

"Casselli believes she is hitchhiking to Rome. There was a line of thunderstorms over most of western Italy last night, so she may have taken shelter someplace, but Casselli has promised to send out his men to find her. When that happens, I will see that she is promptly returned safely to you."

"Thank you, Pietro."

"You owe me no thanks, I am simply helping a father in distress. It will no doubt help if you will pray to God for her safe return, as will I."

"I'll do that, Pietro."

"I'll call you as soon as I hear something. Good night." The cardinal hung up.

Instead of immediately praying for God's help, Arthur called Stone Barrington.

S tone picked up his phone. "Hello, Arthur?"

"Yes, Stone. I have heard that Hedy is alive and well and that she is hitchhiking to Rome."

Arthur is breaking under the pressure, Stone thought.

"I heard this directly from Cardinal Prizzi."

"Cardinal Prizzi? How the hell do you know him?"

"I met him on his last visit to New York. We played golf—he is a fanatic—and I gave him a couple of investment opportunities. We're thinking of collaborating on something."

Stone's mind reeled.

"The cardinal spoke directly to Casselli."

"How did he do that?" Stone asked. "Did he have a direct line?"

"I don't know, but Prizzi knows *everybody*."

"What did Casselli say?"

"He said that Hedy left his house last night and was hitchhiking to Rome."

"We had awful weather last night," Stone said, remembering the rain beating against his window.

"Prizzi postulates that she may have taken shelter along the way. Casselli told him he would send his men out to look for her."

First, the good news, then, the bad. "I'll alert the Italian police," Stone said. "And I'll get back to you when there is news."

"I'll look forward to hearing from you." Both men hung up.

Stone went into the living room, which had become a command post for the DIA and the CIA, and reported the call to Jim and Dante.

Jim stared at him blankly. "Cardinal Prizzi from the Vatican Bank?"

"He's apparently a personal friend of Arthur's."

"So Hedy wasn't lying when she said that Arthur knew the Pope?"

"I doubt that. If Arthur knew the Pope, believe me, he would have called him instead of the cardinal. Dante, is there anything in your file on Casselli that connects him with the Vatican? In particular, with the Vatican Bank?"

Dante turned to his computer and began doing searches. "I have the two of them at the consecration of a private chapel that Casselli's company built for a prominent Napoli Catholic layman. That's it."

Jim spoke up. "The question here is: Who's hallucinating? Arthur? The cardinal? Everybody?"

"Arthur is not the sort to hallucinate," Stone said, "and from what I've heard of Prizzi, neither is he. Casselli, on the other hand . . ."

"No, Jim," Dante said. "The question is: Are we still going to run this infiltration thing, if Hedy isn't in the house anymore?"

"Of course we are," Jim said. "We're not going to rely on Casselli's word that she's left his house."

"And if she is gone, we're going to run this elaborate operation, in order to arrest Casselli for dealing in stolen chocolate? I don't think I could explain that to the minister."

"There is the matter of the kidnapping of both Hedy and Baron Klaucke," Stone pointed out. "And we would have . . . at least one of them to testify."

"Hedy could be dead in a ditch somewhere," Dante said, "and there's little doubt that Casselli could get to Klaucke before he could talk."

"I think we have to stick to best-case scenarios," Jim said, "unless we get more information to the contrary. Dante, can you alert the police between

Amalfi and here to be on the lookout for an American woman?"

"Of course," Dante said, picking up his phone.

"And we're still on for tomorrow night?" Stone asked.

"Yes," Dante said, "we're still on, God help us."

# 51

Hedy kept an intermittent watch on the trail and the house all day, and there was much foot traffic, people and donkeys delivering crates of wine, food, flowers, and anonymous cartons. She managed to snatch two oranges from another donkey, but she was very, very hungry.

Night came, but activity still continued in the kitchen, at the rear of the house, until after midnight. Finally, at around two AM, the house went quiet. Hedy crept out of her hiding place and padded down the trail to the rear deck, where she peered through the available windows for signs of life. Nothing.

She used her key to let herself in the rear door, leaving it unlocked for a quick escape; there was a night-light in the kitchen, which allowed her to see her way. She snatched a canvas shopping bag from a counter, went to the refrigerator and filled it with salami, ham, and cheeses and a bottle of San Pellegrino sparkling water, tucking a loaf of bread in with them.

She turned to go and spotted something that made her heart leap: an iPhone on the counter, plugged in and charging. She got out her dead phone and unplugged the other. Her heart sank: it was an older model, with the multiple pin connector. Hers was new and used the smaller plug. She turned on the phone and tried to use it, but she didn't have the password. Sadly, she plugged it back in again and tucked away her own phone.

In the back hall she found cases of wine stacked up. She grabbed a bottle of red, let herself out of the house, locked the door behind her, and returned to her hideaway, where she opened the wine with the corkscrew in her pocket and washed down cheese, bread, and meat until she was replete and more than a little drunk.

She berated herself for leaving the house so quickly, when there must be things there she could use, like a flashlight. Emboldened by the wine, she went back into the house and began to search again, going through all the kitchen drawers. No flashlight.

That done, she tiptoed into the huge living room, where she had been dragged to see Casselli before. She went carefully through the whole room by the light of a single lamp left on, and found not only no flashlight, but nothing else of use to her, except a cashmere blanket hung over a sofa. That, she tucked under her arm, then left the house again. She had been afraid to use the landline phones in the house, for fear of rousing someone, and anyway, she didn't know any useful dialing codes.

She finished the bottle of wine and, wrapped cozily in the cashmere, fell soundly asleep, determined to make her way out of there on the morrow.

Casselli was going crazy. Every few minutes he got a report from his people who were out searching for Hedy, and every one was the same: no sight of her. He grew hoarse, screaming down the phone, and then the dreaded call came.

"All right, Casselli, where is the girl?" the cardinal demanded.

"I beg you to believe me, Your Eminence, we have not been able to locate her. Has no one heard from her?"

"No one, and you are going to hell."

"I have doubled the number of men searching for her," Casselli said, weeping. "I pray God will protect her."

"He will not protect you from me," the cardinal said, and hung up.

Casselli's secretary rushed into the room, frightened by the wailing noises coming from her boss. She had never seen him like this; no one had.

Hedy slept soundly until midday, and awoke with a hangover. She drank some of the fizzy water, then had a good lunch. First chance, she would steal another bottle of wine. Hair of the dog.

The trail still brought a steady stream of men and donkeys. There must be a party tonight, she thought. And she had nothing to wear!

At mid-morning, a makeup artist from the Rome station came and surveyed Stone's face. She clipped a sample of his hair. "You could use a haircut," she said to him. "Want me to do it?"

"No, thank you, I am an artiste tonight, and I think the hair suits me."

"Quite right. I'm going to take a bit more, though, for your mustache," and she went about his head, taking a clump here and there. "It will look better if it's made from your own hair," she explained.

Finally, she mixed some plaster, smeared some Vaseline on his nose, and took a cast of the proboscis. "I'll be back later with your new nose," she said.

Stone, Dino, Jim, and Dante's assistant, Guido, spent some time rehearsing that morning, and Stone thought they sounded not half bad.

"Okay," Jim said, "we depart this location at four PM, and remember, it's black-tie."

"Nobody told me," Dino said.

"Told you about what?"

"I didn't bring a tuxedo to Rome."

Dante ordered Guido, their guitarist, to take Dino out and find him a rental.

# 52

Stone got a call late that morning from a number he didn't recognize, but the country code was 44, Britain. "Hello?"

"I have Director Devonshire for you," a man said. "Can you take the call?" Felicity Devonshire was an old friend and sometime lover of Stone's, who was also head of Britain's foreign intelligence service, MI6.

"Of course," Stone said. Then he heard a click and some beeps.

"Stone?"

"Yes, Felicity, how are you?"

"My question is, how are you? In one piece?"

"Why, yes, why wouldn't I be?"

"I've been hearing rumblings about you."

"From where?"

"The Italian DIA, the Agency, and the Vatican Bank, for God's sake."

"You have very sharp ears."

"I have many sharp ears all over Europe," she said.

He didn't doubt that for a moment. "Of course you do. What have you heard?"

"That you're in some sort of rumble with a mobster named Leo Casselli."

"That would be accurate, as far as it goes."

"Why haven't you called me for help?"

"It didn't occur to me to call British intelligence about something happening in Italy."

"And Paris, from what I hear. Do you need anything? Can I help?"

Stone thought about that for a moment. "I think I have all the help I need for the moment. That could change rapidly, though, and if it does, I'll call you, perhaps as soon as tomorrow."

"You have my cell number, do you not?"

"I do."

"I'm going down to the country this afternoon and take a couple of days."

"To Kent?"

"No, to Hampshire. My father had what he called his 'sailing cottage' on the Beaulieu River." She pronounced it "Bewley." "And that reminds me of something: When are you going back to New York?"

"In a few days, I hope. My airplane is here, and I'm flying it home."

"Could you stop off in England for a few days?" she asked. "There's something I want to show you that I think you'll find very interesting."

"And what is that?"

"I'm not going to tell you—it will have to be a surprise."

"Things, as you might imagine, are up in the air here. May I call you when they settle down?"

"You may, but hurry."

"I'll hurry," he said.

"And be careful tonight. I don't like the thought of you with bullet holes in your carcass."

"Neither do I." They said goodbye and hung up.

The others came and sat down around Stone. "We have a problem," Jim said.

"Not another one."

"Yes, and a big one: How are we going to get guns into the house?"

Stone blinked. "You've just thought of that now?"

"This is serious," Dante said. "Casselli is a cautious man. He's going to have people searching everyone who enters the house. We've got five men and one woman who are going to be dressed as waiters: they're smuggling their weapons in wine crates with false bottoms."

"I don't suppose there's room for ours in there?"

"No, and even if there was, they'll be operating out of the kitchen, at the rear of the house, while you'll be playing at the front of the house. They might have trouble getting them to you."

"Why don't we put them in your bass fiddle, Jim?" Stone asked.

"Because they'll rattle around."

Dino spoke up. "You can put them in my snare drum. The head comes off with a key."

"They'll rattle around in there, too," Jim said.

"So wrap them in pieces of soft cloth, like velvet."

"When would you have an opportunity to get them out of the snare?"

"At our first break. Union rules: ten minutes every hour."

Jim shook his head. "We may need them before that."

"All right, I'll get them out of the drum while we're setting up to play. Nobody's going to be paying attention to the band, especially since they will already have searched us on the way in."

"How long will that take?" Jim asked

Dino held up a key. "Let's find out." He went to

where the drums were set up, sat on the stool, and picked up the snare. It took him two minutes to loosen the clamps that held the drumhead on. "There you go. Come and get your guns."

"Okay," Jim said. "We've got a meeting at two-thirty for everybody who's going to be inside the house, so we can coordinate."

Stone began to feel a little nervous. He consoled himself by thinking of Felicity Devonshire and her secret, waiting for him in England.

# 53

Stone went two floors up, to Marcel's roof garden, for some air. The sun was shining, and the view was spectacular. His cell rang. "Hello?"

"It's Joan," his secretary said. "Arthur Steele tried to call you but couldn't get through."

"I don't know why not—everybody else is getting through."

"You don't have to call him back, he just wanted to leave a message."

"Okay."

"He says that your insurance policy with him includes, under liability, up to ten million dollars for ransom money. He stressed that it was a liability clause—the person for whom you're paying the ransom doesn't have to be a spouse or a relative. This is just to cover any liability exposure you might have."

"Trust Arthur to think of that."

"Well, he does run a very large insurance company. I went back and read your policy—he's right."

"I never got that far into the fine print," Stone said. "Who reads his entire insurance policy?"

"Stone, are you in some kind of trouble? Why would you need ransom money?"

"I'll tell you all about it when I get home."

"And when will that be? The mail is piling up here."

"Answer as much of it as you can, then save the rest. If it's a legal matter, send it to Herb Fisher at Woodman & Weld."

"And you're coming home when?"

"Maybe another week. I've got things to clear up here with Marcel, then I may have to stop in England on the way home."

"Do you want me to get Pat Frank to come and fly back with you?"

"Joan, I'm rated as a single pilot, I can handle it."

"If you say so."

"Don't sound so doubtful when you say that."

"I just don't want to have to start looking for a new boss at my age."

"Stop it. Goodbye." He hung up. Immediately, the phone rang again. "Hello?"

"It's Dino. Your makeup person is here. Where the hell are you?"

"Up on the roof."

"Well, get down here."

Stone walked back downstairs and saw Jim and Dino wrapping pistols in cloths and packing them into the snare drum.

The makeup artist, whose name was Marge, was unpacking some things and laying them out on a table. "Come over here and sit down," she said.

Stone walked over and took a seat.

"Okay," Marge said, "let me show you how to put your nose on."

"On, so that it won't come off?"

"Not unless someone rips it off. Avoid that."

She held up a tiny plastic bottle. "This," she said, "is, for want of a better word, glue. It's what insecure men use to stick on their hairpieces." She held up some latex. "This is your nose. Let's try it on, first without glue." She set up a little three-way mirror and then came at Stone with the latex, smoothing the edges. "Just a minute." She got some scissors and did some trimming around the edges. "There, that's good." She applied it to Stone's face and pointed him toward the mirror. "What do you think?"

"Good God!" Stone said, staring at himself. "It looks real."

"Well, of course it looks real, I'm in the business of real. If I get it wrong, people can die."

"Like me?"

"Yeah, like you."

"Well, I don't know who the guy in the mirror is, but his nose looks real to me."

"Good. Now for the glue: watch this, in case you have to make repairs." She applied the glue to the edges of the latex, then came at him again, pressing and stroking the edges. "Now look again."

Stone looked in the mirror. "I can't see the edges."

"That's because I tapered them until they're very thin, so that they sort of disappear into your skin." She picked up something that looked like a poorly made brush. "Now for your mustache: it uses the same glue, and what's more, it conceals the edges of the nose under your nostrils, where they are most likely to be noticed, because your upper lip moves." She put glue onto the back of the mustache and pressed it into place.

Stone looked in the mirror. "It looks awful," he said.

"Of course it does, because I haven't trimmed it." Marge picked up some barber scissors and a fine-toothed comb and made snipping noises for a few minutes. "Now," she said, pointing him at the mirror.

"Ah, much better," Stone said. "I've always wondered what I would look like with a mustache. Now I know. I'll never wear one again after today."

"It looks all the more real because it's your own hair."

"It certainly does."

"Now for the glasses," she said, holding up a pair of wraparound sunglasses. "Notice that they're darker in the middle than at the edges. That will let you use your peripheral vision. If someone looks directly into your eyes, he won't be able to tell where you're looking."

"It's very dark in the middle," Stone said.

"Let me give you a tip," Marge said. "I knew a guy, once, who was almost but not totally blind. He could read a letter, if he held it up to just an inch or two from his eyes. If you get in trouble because you can't see well enough, push the glasses up and hold something close as if to read it. That will give you a chance to look around."

Stone tried it, and it worked.

Marge made some adjustments so that the glasses fit better, then she stood back and looked at her work. "What do you think?"

Stone checked the mirror. "I've never seen that guy before in my life."

"Neither has Leo Casselli."

# 54

Stone got up from his chair and took Marge's arm. "Walk me over to the piano," he said. There was a lot of chatter in the room, and it suddenly died. Stone could see well enough through the dark lenses to know that everyone was looking at him.

He reached out and felt for the piano, then found the chair with his other hand and slid into it. He played a fanfare, then waited. The group burst into applause.

"You look fantastic," Jim said. "If you had walked in here in that disguise, I would have shot you."

"He's right," Dino said. "I wouldn't have known you."

"Neither would I," Stone said, rising and moving

around, still practicing feeling his way. Dino reached out to help him.

"It's okay, Dino, I'm not really blind." Everybody laughed, then they all got very quiet again.

*"Buon giorno,"* a booming voice said. There, standing next to Marcel and dressed in red, stood a cardinal of the Church. He walked over to Stone and made the sign of the cross. "I will say a special prayer for the blind for you." He looked confused when everyone burst out laughing.

Stone took off his glasses. "I'm not really blind, Your Eminence," he said. "It's just for today."

Prizzi joined in the laughter. "And you are Mr. Barrington?"

"I am."

"I bring the regards of Arturo Steele."

"Thank you, Your Eminence. I hope to see him soon."

"I truly believe that Casselli no longer has possession of your lady friend," he said. "He was too frightened to lie to me."

"What was he frightened of?"

"The Church. Like many, he is not devout, but he is superstitious. There are many superstitions about the Church and its priests. Even some people who don't believe think that we have special powers, like witches. Casselli believes I can send him to hell. Only God can do that." He smiled. "But I can wave good-bye to him. Has anyone had sight of the young woman?"

"No, Your Eminence, not yet, but we are hopeful that she will be found soon, perhaps on the road from Amalfi to Rome."

"May God make it so." Then the cardinal began to work the room like a politician, shaking hands and chatting with people. Finally, he made his way toward the elevator, then stopped and turned. "You are all brave men and women," he said, "and I will pray for your success tonight." Then he was gone.

"I wasn't expecting him," Jim said.

"I was," Dante replied. "He asked the minister if he could come and see us off."

Marge packed up her gear, then came back to Stone and gave him an aluminum rod. "This is how it works," she said, unfolding it. "Practice it a few times, and use it tonight—it will lend credibility."

Stone got the hang of it. "Thank you, Marge, for this and for the new nose." He gave her a hug.

"Just do me proud," she said, then left.

Dino began packing up his drums and putting them into their cases, and Stone helped him.

"Would you have believed a week ago that you and I would be playing a gig tonight?" Dino asked.

Stone laughed. "No, I wouldn't have believed that."

"Nice of the cardinal to drop by."

"Yes, it was. First cardinal I ever met. No, that's wrong—I met one in Venice who was all set to marry me to Dolce Bianchi, until Providence intervened."

"Only Providence could have saved you from that fate," Dino said.

The room began filling with people, some in police uniforms, some in waiters' clothes, and some in suits. Introductions were made, and hands were shaken.

Stone and Dino went to their respective rooms to change into their tuxedos.

When they came back into the living room a large screen had been set up, and the group had arranged themselves around the room, some of them on the floor.

Mike Freeman got off the elevator, and someone pointed out Stone.

Mike came over. "Is it you, Stone?"

"You must have me confused with someone else," Stone said. "I am the blind pianist."

"I recognize the voice," he said, laughing. "I hear you're the entertainment tonight."

"Dino and I, plus Jim Lugano and Guido, our guitarist. Until the shooting starts."

"I hope there won't be any shooting."

"We can all hope," Stone replied.

# 55

Dante called the group to order. "I will speak in English," he said, "since you are all conversant in the language." He clicked a remote control, and a photograph of the Casselli house appeared on the screen. Clearly taken from the air, it showed everything from the roof down past the Amalfi drive to the sea. "This is our target," Dante said. He pressed a button and the camera zoomed in and moved up, until they had a bird's-eye view.

"Here," he said, pointing to the rear deck, "is a platform marked on the plans as a helicopter landing pad. We had originally intended to set down a troop-carrying naval chopper there with twenty-five men aboard. However, we are cursed with winds forecast for tonight of more than thirty knots, and there is so little room for error that we have decided to bus in our backup to the village square in Ravello. Our troops will then walk about a kilometer down this narrow path, which ends at the chopper platform. It will be dark, the path is narrow, with only a rope handrail for safety, and the drop to the bottom is steep, ranging between fifty and one hundred meters, so they must use their flashlights and be very careful. It will be slow going. The path widens as it approaches the deck. Four men will be assigned to rush the deck and take any security people who might be stationed there. They will be carrying silenced weapons.

"Now, the other point of entry: from the Amalfi drive at the front of the house." The image on the screen moved and the camera descended to the road. "Behind this high hedge is the entrance to the elevator, which is large, three by three meters. This will certainly be guarded, and it is likely that all guests will be searched or wanded for weapons. Around a curve a hundred meters away we will have twenty-five more men in a bus."

He switched to the blueprints and highlighted the living room. "This room is very large and was built for entertaining. The caterers inform us that fifty-eight people will be served dinner, about equally divided between men and women. There will be several armed security guards in the house, and we have learned that they will be wearing dark suits and identified by large lapel buttons bearing the letter *C*. We believe that the guards downstairs will have served us by disarming all the guests, therefore, the security guards are our wild cards: if shooting erupts, it will be from them, so those of you stationed inside the house should identify them from their lapel pins and make them your first targets, if necessary. The next target will be Leo Casselli himself, who should be taken alive, if at all possible, and you have all seen photographs of him. On past social occasions hosted by Casselli, he has worn a white dinner jacket, so that may help you to immediately identify him.

"The four members of the band will arrive at the Amalfi drive entrance to the house, where they will probably be searched, then taken up in the elevator. The piano is situated at the Amalfi end of the living room, near the elevator, so we believe the band will be put there.

"There will be twelve people in waiters' uniforms. Those working for the caterers will be wearing white jackets. Our people, five of them, will be wearing red jackets. All the catering personnel, who are already en route, will arrive at the square in Ravello in their own vans and a small bus. They will be the first to arrive, in daylight, and after dark, they will walk down the narrow path from the square and enter the house through the rear door on command. All the food, wine, and utensils will have already been delivered to the kitchen, which is of a large and commercial nature. Two of these crates have been marked with a large red *C*. These have false bottoms and contain the weapons to be used by our five people— four men and one woman. They will also contain three Tasers. These will be used to disable and disarm the security personnel, probably two, who work on the lower floor here." The image changed to the plan of the lower floor. "This room contains audio and video equipment connected to the many cameras around the house and property. At seven PM, as the guests have begun to arrive, two of our waiters in red jackets, armed with Tasers and pistols, will go to the security room, Tase the occupants, and immobilize them with plastic cuffs on their hands and feet, and they will also gag these people. Their pistols will be silenced. They may have to be fired, depending on the level of resistance. At the same time, our female officer will go to the lower level where four maids' rooms are located. We believe that Hedy Kiesler may be held in one of these rooms, though we've had reports that she is no longer in the house. We have to find out. Three of them should be unoccupied, since their occupants will be upstairs, working. Our woman will be carrying a jimmy bar with which to force the doors, if locked.

"Having reached Hedy, our officer will remain in the room with her until the house has been secured, when another of our people will come for them and walk them to the elevator for extraction from the house. It is possible that Hedy has already left or been taken from the house to another location, in which case we will have another problem on our hands. If so, the security people and staff of the house will be aggressively interrogated as to Hedy's whereabouts.

"All our inside people, including the musicians, will be equipped with earpieces that contain two-way radios. Commands will be given by these means, and people who have no critical information for everyone else should remain silent.

"Darkness will fall at around seven PM. At approximately seven-thirty to seven forty-five, our guitarist, Guido, will make an announcement, using a microphone attached to his guitar's amplifier. The other musicians will have earlier retrieved their weapons from the snare drum and will be ready. Guido will announce that they are all under arrest and surrounded. He will reassure them that, after being interviewed, nearly all the guests will be released and allowed to leave. The band members will be responsible for detaining Leo Casselli."

Stone raised his hand. "Dante, may I make a suggestion?"

"Yes, Stone, of course."

"Perhaps Guido, before he makes his announcement of arrest, could ask Casselli to come to the microphone and welcome his guests. That way, he will detach himself from the crowd, so we will know where he is, and while Guido makes his announcement, we can cuff Casselli, take him down in the elevator, and put him into a vehicle. I assume that the downstairs guards will have already been taken."

"Yes, they will be in custody by that time, and I accept your suggestion, which is an excellent one. You, Stone, may have the pleasure of taking Casselli." There was applause in the room.

"And now, are there any questions? No? Then you will all be in your assigned vehicles at four PM. Waiters, please go now, since you need a head start."

The meeting broke up, and everyone went to his assigned vehicle. The band members were assigned to a van, inside which the neck of the bass fiddle protruded into the passenger compartment.

Stone took his seat. In a moment, they were off.

# 56

Hedy had run out of food and wine as the day waned, and two security guards now manned the rear deck, so she could not get into the house or leave her hiding place without being seen. She resolved that once darkness fell, she would leave her nest among the rocks and make her way up the path toward wherever it led, regardless of the danger. She would crawl, if necessary, but she would do it. Irrationally, she began to blame Stone for her predicament, and her single-minded goal in getting out became confronting him with her many complaints. She longed to be back in New York, where no one wished to kidnap or otherwise harm her. Italy no longer seemed an attractive place to live and work.

\*　　\*　　\*

The van carrying the musicians made its way, by necessity slowly, down the Amalfi drive, past the Casselli house, and around a bend, where it made a U-turn in a wide place in the road and parked. Daylight was waning, and it would soon be dark.

Everyone except Stone had been chatty on the drive down from Rome, but now an uncommanded silence fell on the little group. Dante, who was their driver, got out his radios and began contacting his various units, inside and outside the house. As the hour neared six-thirty, he announced to his passengers, "All groups are in place. It is time for the band to arrive and begin setting up. Four of our people will arrive in a limousine in less than an hour, and after you and all the guests go up in the elevator, they will take the security guards stationed there. On your ride up in the elevator you will no doubt be seen on video and heard on audio by the men manning the security room, so don't say anything that would disturb them. Please place your radio in your left ear and listen for transmissions, then count off by instrument, so that I know I can receive you. Jim, call me when the band is in place, and give me a report on conditions in the living room."

Everyone did as instructed, then Dante started the van and drove around the corner to the parking area adjoining the house. Stone helped Dino unload his drums in their cases and load them into the elevator. Each man had a wand passed over his body to ensure he had no weapons. The two security men looked inside the drum cases, but not inside the drums.

"Ted," Jim said, using Stone's assigned name, as they stepped out of the elevator, "I wish you could see this room and the view—both are spectacular." He led Stone to the piano, and Stone felt his way around it, opening the lid to the first position, then sitting at the keyboard and playing a few chords. It was a nine-foot Steinway concert grand, the first he had ever played.

Dino, assisted by Jim, unpacked his drums, then knelt behind the bass to open the snare drum and distribute the weapons and spare magazines. Jim stood behind Stone and leaned over as if speaking to him, then tucked the 9mm semiautomatic into his cummerbund and slipped the spare magazine into his pocket. "There's one in the chamber," he whispered, "and the safety is on. You are now armed, Ted."

Dino quickly reassembled the snare drum and arranged his drums and his stool, then did some final tuning of each drum.

Guido found a receptacle to plug in his amp, and

Stone gave them a *C* to tune the stringed instruments by, then they were ready.

Jim spoke without moving his lips. "Dante, the band is in place, and all is well. Guests are being brought upstairs in carloads and are being served drinks and canapés. Three of our red jackets are circulating among the guests. I can see four security guards. Mr. C is not yet in view."

"Roger," Dante repeated.

"Ted, it's seven o'clock," Jim said. "Count us off."

Stone did so, and they swung into a medium-tempo version of "C Jam Blues," to loosen up everybody and get them accustomed to playing together. Stone held his head still, so as not to appear to be watching his hands or looking around. With his peripheral vision he could see the formally dressed and bejeweled crowd. With the end of the number he led the group into a ballad, and some of the guests began dancing.

"Seven-fifteen," Dante said. "All is on schedule. The number of arriving guests is declining. I count forty-six present, twelve still to arrive."

Suddenly, a man in a white dinner jacket was standing next to Stone, and there was a hand on his shoulder. He flinched a little.

"Sorry to startle you," Casselli said. "I just want to tell you the band sounds wonderful."

*"Mille grazie,"* Stone replied, and continued to play.

Another quarter of an hour passed, and a woman's voice was heard over the radio. "Hedy is not present in any of the maids' rooms," she said. "Nor have we found her anywhere in the house. The security room has been taken and three occupants immobilized and drugged."

"Roger," Dante replied. "Guido, as soon as our three officers rejoin the others, you may begin the operation. The time is up to you. Announce your intentions when ready, and give us a countdown."

"Roger wilco," Guido replied. "Mr. C is in the room, and he likes the music."

Stone heard all this, and his pulse quickened.

# 57

They finished playing the number, and Guido set down his guitar in its stand and stepped forward to the microphone. Stone and Dino provided a little fanfare to quiet the crowd.

"Good evening, ladies and gentlemen," Guido said. "I'm sure your host, Signor Casselli, would like to say a few words of welcome to you." There was loud applause, and Guido beckoned Casselli to the microphone and stepped back.

Casselli gave a modest little wave to the group. "Good evening to all of you. It is my great pleasure to welcome you to my new home, and I hope this will be the first of your many visits." The crowd applauded again. "Also, I would just like to mention that my former residence in Positano is available for purchase." That got a laugh and another round of applause. Before the noise could die down, Guido stepped forward and pressed his gun against Casselli's spine. "There is a gun in your back," he whispered into his ear. "You are under arrest. Do exactly as I say, or you will be shot. Put your hands behind you."

Stone took off his dark glasses, stood up, and went to Casselli. He grabbed his hands and pulled them behind his back, while Guido applied the plastic tie. The room fell quiet, and then all hell broke loose.

A security guard produced a weapon, pointed it at them, and yelled, "Let him go and step back!" Dino, from his perch behind the drums, stood up, assumed a combat stance, and shot the guard in the chest. At the sound of the shot the crowd began to scream and to try to get out.

Stone and Guido dragged Casselli backward toward the elevator, while Dino and Jim pointed their weapons at the guests and tried to keep them back. Stone and Guido got Casselli onto the elevator and pressed the down button; nothing happened, then the lights went out in the whole house. Pandemonium ensued. Dim emergency lighting came on, and in the dimness the crowd tried to push back against Jim and Dino. Jim fired two rounds into the ceiling, and they stepped back for a moment. Then there was the sound of an engine cranking somewhere outside the house, and the generator started to work. The lights came on, the elevator doors closed, and they started down.

"Good evening, Mr. Casselli," Stone said, facing the man.

"Who are you?" Casselli demanded. "And what are you doing?"

"We last met in Paris," Stone said. "Remember the *choucroute*?"

"Barrington?"

"Yes. And to answer your question, I am assisting the police in your arrest and detention. Now where is Hedy?"

"I don't know," Casselli said.

Stone pressed his pistol against Casselli's right eye. "Just one more time: Where is Hedy?"

"She left my house two nights ago, after she spoke to you on the phone. We have not been able to find her. That is the truth."

The elevator stopped on the ground floor, and they hustled Casselli out the door, around the hedge, and into a waiting car, next to a policeman. Stone slammed the door. "Enjoy the ride," he yelled at Casselli, then he turned to the others. "I think we're needed upstairs," he said.

Dante joined them, pistol drawn, and they got

back into the elevator and rose. They burst into the living room, weapons out in front of them. The guests were all sitting on the floor, their hands on top of their heads. There was gunfire from the rear, toward the kitchens, and Dante led the way toward the gunfire. Another security guard was lying at the entrance to the kitchen with a head wound, and an officer in a red jacket was bleeding from a leg and being attended to by a colleague. Uniformed policemen were now pouring into the house.

Hedy peeked over a rock and watched, astonished, as the uniforms crowded into the house. A higher ranking officer was behind them, exhorting them to get inside. She climbed over the rocks and ran toward the house, crossing the deck and catching up with the officer as he entered the house. She tapped him rudely on the shoulder, and he spun around.

"I am Hedy Kiesler. Are you looking for me?"

Inside, a semblance of order had been restored. "Who turned off the power?" Dante was yelling.

"We don't know," one of the red-jacketed waiters replied. "Perhaps one of the guards in the security post downstairs."

"Attend to them at once!" Dante shouted.

Stone was standing behind him, looking into the living room full of people on the floor. Guido had taken the microphone again. "All women, get up and come to the elevator," he announced. "The men will go later." Reluctantly, the women began to move.

Stone was watching this happen when someone took him by the shoulder and spun him around, then he caught a fist in his new nose.

"Oh, I'm sorry," Hedy said, looking appalled. "I thought you were someone else."

Stone pulled off his latex nose. "Want another swing?" he asked, then ducked as it came.

# 58

Stone blocked her swing and caught her wrist, then pulled off his mustache. "Am I more familiar, now?" She started to swing again, but he caught her wrists and pinned her arms to her sides and shouted, "Stop it! What are you doing?"

"You miserable bastard!" Hedy shouted back. "Where have you been? I've been living rough outside for two nights!"

"Stop struggling, relax, and listen to me," Stone said.

Reluctantly, she did so. "All right, explain."

"We were unable to confirm your location until very recently."

"That's a lie! I told you where I was in my first text!"

"You said only that you were on a coast."

"I said I was on the *A* coast!"

Stone was baffled, then he got it. *"The A coast?"*

"Yes!"

"I'm sorry, we didn't get that, the big *A*."

"I've been living under a rock. I got out of my room during the night after I talked to you on the phone."

"That was the night we figured it out. Look, we'll sit down tomorrow after you've had a bath and a good night's sleep, and I'll take you through everything we did to find you."

"Are you saying I need a *bath?"* Her voice was rising again.

"Well, yes, don't you think so? Just tell me what you want, Hedy, and I'll arrange it. Just tell me."

"All right: I want to be driven back to Rome right now. I want to go to my apartment, where I can have the bath I apparently need so much, and pack my things. I want to be on a plane for New York tomorrow afternoon. Can you handle all that?"

"Just a moment," Stone said, and snagged the passing Dante. He explained what Hedy needed.

"All right," Dante said. "Do you have a passport?"

Hedy looked nonplussed. "No, it's in Paris, in my handbag, in Stone's house."

"All right, someone will drive you to Rome now. You'll be picked up tomorrow morning at eleven

313

o'clock and driven to the American Embassy, which will issue you a new passport, then you will be driven to the airport. I'll see that you have a seat on the two PM Alitalia flight to New York, and that a ticket is waiting for you. Is that satisfactory?"

"*Most* satisfactory," Hedy said.

"You must remember that you will need to return to Rome for Casselli's trial, in a few months."

"All right, if I have to."

"I'll have your things at my Paris house over-nighted to New York tomorrow," Stone said. He handed her his telephone. "Now call Arthur."

She took the phone and walked a few steps away. "How do I call the States?" she asked. Stone gave her the code. She was apparently connected quickly, because she spent the next three minutes talking rapidly, then hung up and handed Stone his phone. "Arthur is having me met."

"Is there anything else I can do for you?" Stone asked.

"I'll let you know if I think of something."

"You have my number. Do you still have your cell phone?"

"Yes," she said, patting her pocket. "And you wouldn't believe where it's been."

Dante stepped up with his female officer. "This is

Maria. She will drive you to Rome and your apartment. Are you ready to go?"

"I can't tell you how happy I am to go," she said. She grabbed a plate of food and a glass of wine from a kitchen counter. "Let's go, Maria."

Stone and Dante watched them walk to the elevator and go down. "What was that all about?" Dante asked.

"Hedy felt that we had taken too long to find her. I'll explain it all tomorrow, if she's speaking to me."

"I wouldn't count on that," Dante said. "She's pretty angry."

"What's going on over there?" Stone asked. Two of his men were sitting at the dining table, speaking to one of the male guests.

"We're identifying all the men and checking our computer for arrest warrants. At the very least, we'll be charging them with associating with criminals—that is, Casselli and the other guests. I believe we'll net a couple of dozen convictions from this crowd."

Dino walked up. "What's going on? I just saw Hedy leave with a policewoman."

"She's upset with me, says I didn't do enough to find her quickly."

Dino shook his head. "Are you ready to get out of here? I don't think they need us anymore."

"I'll get someone to drive you," Dante said.

"It's a pity you didn't speak up sooner," Stone said. "We could have ridden with Hedy."

Dino laughed. "From the look of her, she'd probably go for my gun."

"What about your drums?"

"I gave them to Guido—they're his problem now."

"Viv will be so relieved."

# 59

There was no one available to drive them, so they were given a car with a GPS and Dino drove.

"So, what are your plans now?" he asked Stone.

"Tomorrow, I'm going to go over the hotel plans with Marcel, and see if there's anything else to help him with. The day after, I'm going to fly the airplane to England. I have an invitation from Felicity Devonshire. She says she's got something she wants to show me."

"Yeah, I'll bet she does."

"Something besides that."

"What?"

"I don't know—she says it's a secret."

"And you're willing to fly to England for that?"

"It's got to be important, or she wouldn't have

insisted I come. Anyway, it'll be nice to see her, especially since Hedy is never going to speak to me again."

"And after that?"

"I'll fly the airplane back to Teterboro, via Lisbon and the Azores. I should be back by the end of the week, at the most. Are you leaving tomorrow?"

"I spoke to Viv. She's making our travel arrangements now."

"You might be on the airplane with Hedy," Stone pointed out. "Dante is putting her on the Alitalia flight at two PM."

"That's our flight, I think."

"If you get the opportunity, tell Hedy what we've been doing for the past few days, will you?"

"I'll let Viv handle that, I think."

"Smart move."

It was past midnight before they were back at Marcel's place and in their beds.

The following morning Stone called Felicity, and he was put through immediately by her assistant.

"Hello, there."

"Hi. I can be there tomorrow, if that's okay."

"Wonderful. Do you have a dinner jacket with you?"

"Yes, I played in a band last night. I'll tell you all about it."

"Good. We'll go across the Solent and have dinner at the Royal Yacht Squadron. There's someone I want you to meet who'll be dining with us."

"You're not handing me off to another woman, are you?"

"Perish the thought. What time will you arrive?"

"Where should I land?"

"At Southampton. I'll arrange hangar space and fuel for you."

"Okay. Shall we say two PM?"

"I'll meet you on the ramp at Signature Flight Support, and I'll arrange your prior permission to land. What's your tail number?"

"November One Two Three Tango Foxtrot."

"See you then." She hung up, before he could ask about the secret.

Stone went downstairs and found Marcel in his office. "I'm sorry about the past few days," he said, "all those people in your apartment."

"Not at all," Marcel said. "I'm just glad everything turned out so well."

"How are things proceeding with the hotel?"

"Suddenly very well. I tell you the truth, if that

had turned out to be Hedy's finger in that box, I would have walked away from everything here."

"I'm glad it wasn't."

Marcel took him through a list of things he was getting done at the building site. "By tomorrow, we'll be under construction again. Grand opening in about ten months. We'll set a date when we're further along."

"Sounds good. I expect I'll have to come back for Casselli's trial at some point."

"You will always be a welcome guest here. What are your plans now?"

"If you don't need me further, I'll fly to England tomorrow morning to visit a friend for a few days, then on to New York, via Lisbon and the Azores."

"You have the range for that?"

"Ample range, 1,850 miles, 2,000 if I use less than full cruise power. Don't worry."

"You'll be alone?"

"I've done a lot of flying alone. I'll be just fine."

"Whatever you say, my friend. Now let's go upstairs, say goodbye to Dino and Vivian, and have some lunch."

"Good idea," Stone replied, and followed him to the elevator.

# 60

S tone landed his airplane at Southampton Airport, in England, and taxied to the FBO, Signature Aviation. As he came to a halt and shut down his engines, an Aston Martin coupe drew up alongside the airplane, closely followed by a sinister-looking black Range Rover with darkened windows, as was Felicity's due as director of MI6, the British foreign intelligence service. As Stone opened the cabin door and came down the steps, Dame Felicity Devonshire got out of the Aston Martin and flung herself into his arms.

After a kiss and a hug, Stone stowed the cabin steps, closed and locked the door, and got his bags out of the forward luggage compartment. A man in a dark suit got out of the Range Rover, took his luggage, and stowed it in the SUV.

"What airplane is this?" Felicity asked.

"The new one: a Citation CJ3 Plus."

"I love the paint job."

"Thanks, it's my own. You can always spot me on a ramp by the stars on the tail." He walked around the car. "And what Aston Martin is this?"

"It's the DBS, brand-new. I recently sold my father's estate in Kent, so I splurged."

"You certainly did." Stone got into the passenger seat. "I should check in at the FBO."

"Don't bother, it's taken care of. They'll put it in the hangar straightaway and refuel it whenever you like."

"So what's the big surprise?"

"You'll have to wait a little while and take a boat ride, before all is revealed." She drove quickly out of town and onto a motorway for a short distance, which she covered in record time. Soon they were driving through the village of Beaulieu, then down the eastern side of the Beaulieu River, a tidal estuary that flowed into the Solent, the body of water separating the Isle of Wight from the mainland. Soon she used a remote control to open a wrought iron gate, hung on old stone pillars, and drove down a driveway lined by ancient trees until a large stone cottage with a slate roof revealed itself.

"Come with me," she said. "My housekeeper will

take your bags upstairs and press your dinner suit." She led him through a handsomely decorated living room and out a rear door, and they walked down a stone path to a dock, where a charming old wooden cabin cruiser was moored. She got the engines started while Stone dealt with the lines, and they proceeded downstream half a mile and tied up at another dock, where a sign read WINDWARD HALL. They walked up from the floating pontoon and were met by a man in an electric vehicle who took them down a shaded drive.

"Stop here, Stan," Felicity said. "Come on, Stone, we'll walk."

Stone got down from the cart and followed her farther along the narrow road. Without warning they emerged from the trees, and there before them, in a lovely meadow, dotted with old oaks and half a dozen grazing horses, was the most beautiful Georgian house Stone had ever seen. It was large and symmetrical, with wings extending from either side. In the center was a white portico supported by four slender columns. Stone's breath was taken away. "I've never seen anything so perfect," he said.

"That was my reaction, too, when I first saw this house as a child. The owner was a friend of my father's."

"Who lives here?"

"Sir Charles Bourne," she said. "Come, let's go inside."

"Is he expecting us?"

"He's in London this afternoon. He'll join us for dinner at the Royal Yacht Squadron in Cowes tonight, but someone else is expecting us." They walked up the steps, and the door was opened by a butler in his shirtsleeves and an apron, who stuffed a cleaning cloth into his pocket. "Hello, Geoffrey," she said. "This is Mr. Barrington. He's come to see the house."

"Of course, Dame Felicity," the man said in a beautifully modulated voice. "Ms. Blackburn is in the library. Shall I escort you?"

"No, Geoffrey, we'll find our way." They entered a central hall; the pictures had been removed, and scaffolding set up. "It's undergoing a major renovation, which is not yet quite done," she said, showing him a drawing room to his left and a library to his right, which had had all the books removed. "He's having many of the books rebound at a country bindery nearby, and the paneling sanded with two new coats of varnish. There are probably ten or twelve coats present already."

Another woman walked into the room, bearing a canvas carryall and a large drawing pad.

"Stone, this is Susan Blackburn, one of Britain's finest interior designers."

Stone took her hand. "I know your work from pictures in magazines," he said. "It's a pleasure."

"How do you do, Mr. Barrington?" she said coolly. She was tall, perhaps five-ten, and was wearing jeans and a chambray work shirt. Somehow, she made the clothes look elegant.

"Susan, will you show us what you're doing?"

"Of course." She walked them through the library and the drawing room, then took them to a lovely old kitchen with brand-new appliances, then upstairs and to the master suite, which was without furniture or curtains. "We've taken a small bedroom next door and turned it into a dressing room and bath, so there will be two of each. I think that arrangement preserves relationships."

"I agree," Stone said. "I have a similar arrangement in my New York house."

"There are four other bedrooms, each with en suite baths. The present house is the third on a very old property and was built in the 1920s. During the war, the RAF requisitioned it for a bomber base. They didn't give it up until the sixties. Sir Charles bought the place at that time and gave it a thorough systems upgrade, and all mod cons were installed, even air conditioning. The house got pretty run-down and is now undergoing its first full renovation since that time." Some of the rooms were very nearly complete and Stone was impressed with the beauty of the fabrics and wallpapers the designer had employed. "The original estate was more than two thousand acres, in the eighteenth century, but now it's only around a hundred and twenty. There are four cottages, a stable, and a greenhouse on the property."

They spent an hour seeing the house and the beautifully tended gardens. "The renovation is on schedule to be completed in six months' time," Susan said. "Sir Charles has moved into one of the cottages for the duration. Now, if you'll forgive me, I have to return to London for a meeting." She shook hands and departed.

"There's one more thing I want to show you," Felicity said. She took him back to the waiting cart, and they drove half a mile or so, through a grove of large trees, and emerged into a wide space bisected by a runway.

"I didn't know Brits had private airfields," Stone said.

"As Susan said, the RAF built it as a bomber base during the war, and Charles has maintained it as a fully functioning airfield. It even has a published GPS instrument approach, I'm told. Charles owned and flew a King Air, which he has recently sold."

"Is he getting too old to fly?"

"Too ill," Felicity said. "His doctors have given him only a few months to live. You wouldn't know it to see him, but he's really quite sick: his heart. They've told him that when the end comes, it will come quickly."

"I'm very sorry to hear that," Stone said. "It's sad that he won't get to enjoy the house when the work is complete."

"Yes, it is."

"Does he have family who will inherit?"

"He has a son and a daughter from whom he has been estranged for at least twenty years. Both are childless, and he won't leave the house to the National Trust, which he regards as some sort of communist institution that robs the wealthy of their property."

Stone waved a hand. "And this is your secret?"

"Not anymore."

"And why are you showing it to me?"

"Because I expect you to buy the place."

To be continued . . .

# AUTHOR'S NOTE

I am happy to hear from readers, but you should know that if you write to me in care of my publisher, three to six months will pass before I receive your letter, and when it finally arrives it will be one among many, and I will not be able to reply.

However, if you have access to the Internet, you may visit my website at www.stuartwoods.com, where there is a button for sending me e-mail. So far, I have been able to reply to all my e-mail, and I will continue to try to do so.

If you send me an e-mail and do not receive a reply, it is probably because you are among an alarming number of people who have entered their e-mail address incorrectly in their mail software. I have many of my replies returned as undeliverable.

Remember: e-mail, reply; snail mail, no reply.

When you e-mail, please do not send attachments, as I never open these. They can take twenty minutes to download, and they often contain viruses.

Please do not place me on your mailing lists for funny stories, prayers, political causes, charitable fund-raising, petitions, or sentimental claptrap. I get enough of that from people I already know. Generally speaking, when I get e-mail addressed to a large number of people, I immediately delete it without reading it.

Please do not send me your ideas for a book, as I have a policy of writing only what I myself invent. If you send me story ideas, I will immediately delete them without reading them. If you have a good idea for a book, write it yourself, but I will not be able to advise you on how to get it published. Buy a copy of *Writer's Market* at any bookstore; that will tell you how.

Anyone with a request concerning events or appearances may e-mail it to me or send it to: Publicity Department, Penguin Random House, 375 Hudson Street, New York, NY 10014.

Those ambitious folk who wish to buy film, dramatic, or television rights to my books should contact Matthew Snyder, Creative Artists Agency, 9830 Wilshire Boulevard, Beverly Hills, CA 98212-1825.

Those who wish to make offers for rights of a literary nature should contact Anne Sibbald, Janklow & Nesbit, 445 Park Avenue, New York, NY 10022. (Note: This is not an invitation for you to send her your manuscript or to solicit her to be your agent.)

If you want to know if I will be signing books in your city, please visit my website, www.stuartwoods .com, where the tour schedule will be published a month or so in advance. If you wish me to do a book signing in your locality, ask your favorite bookseller to contact his Penguin representative or the Penguin publicity department with the request.

If you find typographical or editorial errors in my book and feel an irresistible urge to tell someone, please write to Sara Minnich at Penguin's address above. Do not e-mail your discoveries to me, as I will already have learned about them from others.

A list of my published works appears in the front of this book and on my website. All the novels are still in print in paperback and can be found at or ordered from any bookstore. If you wish to obtain hardcover copies of earlier novels or of the two nonfiction books, a good used-book store or one of the online bookstores can help you find them. Otherwise, you will have to go to a great many garage sales.

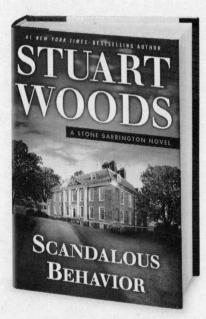

They sat before a fire with a drink as the day waned, dressed for dinner. Stone had not reacted to Felicity's suggestion that he should buy the place, but while he was showering and dressing he could not think of anything else.

"Let me tell you all I know," Felicity said when they were settled.

"Please do."

"Charles has a very carefully thought-out plan: he and his children despise each other. There's no point in going into that history, but he says that if his son inherited he would immediately apply for planning permission to build two hundred awful cottages on the property, and Charles won't have that. He says that his daughter would redecorate the house garishly and sell it to the first person to make a reasonable offer, without regard to what sort of person that might be. Charles, like many Englishmen of his generation and his class, has a long list of persons in mind who qualify as unsuitable, among them Arabs and Russians, who are driving the market in expensive properties these days. Fortunately, Beaulieu is too far from London to have attracted their attention.

"Charles knows that if he dies owning the house, no matter who he leaves it to, a battle will ensue between his children and the unfortunate inheritor. Therefore, he wants to sell it prior to his death to keep it out of their hands, retaining a lifetime tenancy. As I have pointed out, that will likely be no more than a few months.

"You have a number of qualities that would cause Charles to consider you an attractive buyer: One, he would prefer an American gentleman to an unsuitable English spiv, that is, a flashy person of dubious means, who, to Charles's way of thinking, doesn't deserve the money he has somehow made. Two, you are clearly a gentleman, one with an affinity for things English, who will turn up tonight in a dinner suit, instead of a boldly striped nightmare. Three, you are already a person of considerable property, which indicates to Charles that you know how to manage it. Four, you fly an airplane, and he would hate to see his airfield meet the plow. And five, you can write a check for the property, with no delays for obtaining financing or other burdensome requirements that give the opportunity for local gossip, which he has always despised. He would like to sell it as quietly as possible, then present his neighbors and his children with a fait accompli."

"And how large a check would Sir Charles expect me to write?"

"Ten million pounds, and let me remind you that the pound is down against the dollar. I need hardly tell you that that constitutes a screaming bargain in this market, especially with the fresh renovation."

"I should think he could get twice that," Stone observed.

"Yes, but you're not reckoning on Charles's way of calculating. What he wants is the house in proper hands, with the renovation and death duties paid and his loyal staff kept on, and a bit left over for distribution to a few charities he is fond of. Of course, he has other wealth—investments in stocks and business properties in London—but that doesn't come into the equation."

"How many staff?"

"A butler, a cook, and a property manager, and five others in the house, and eight or ten on the property—gardeners, stablemen, and laborers. He would like it if his horses lived out their lives on the estate, but he won't insist."

"Think about this carefully, Felicity, before you answer: Is there a catch in all this?"

Felicity laughed. "Two: his son and daughter will go out of their way to spread awful rumors about you, and you'll have to put up with me as a neighbor."

Stone laughed. "I think I can handle that."

"I'll defend you to the neighbors, and since I'm in London most of the time, anyway, I won't care who you sleep with. You'll have to buy me dinner now and then, though."

With the sun sinking, Felicity took them down the Beaulieu River and across the Solent. There was little wind, and the sea was calm. They fetched up at the little marina maintained by the Royal Yacht Squadron. A tall, slender man in a beautifully cut suit awaited them and helped Felicity ashore, while a uniformed boatman took their lines.

"Charles," Felicity said, "allow me to introduce you to Stone Barrington, of New York. Stone, this is Sir Charles Bourne."

Both men said, "How do you do," simultaneously, then they walked up the path to an old stone castle nestled close by the Solent. Sir Charles took them into a comfortable sitting room and rang for a steward, who took their drinks order. "Please give me a moment to change," Charles said. "I'm fresh off the ferry from Southampton." He vanished.

"Sir Charles seems to be everything he should be," Stone said.

"He thinks the same of you," Felicity replied. "I can tell. An upper-class English gentleman can feign a chilly warmth, but an Englishwoman will know the real thing when she sees it."

"This is quite a place," Stone said, looking around.

"The castle was built by Henry the Eighth, to repel the odious French, who never showed up. The Squadron is celebrating its bicentennial, having been founded in 1815, and is the second-oldest yacht club in the world, after the Royal Cork, which goes back to 1720. Sir Charles and I were practically born into it, both of us having fathers and grandfathers who were members. I was a Lady Associate member, until women were accepted as full members, and I became one of the first."

Sir Charles returned, dressed in a Squadron Mess Kit, in the naval style.

"Well, now, Mr. Barrington," he said, "are you enjoying your stay in England?"

"Please, it's Stone, and I am very much enjoying my stay, although I arrived only this afternoon. I spent much of it enjoying your very beautiful property."

"I'm sorry it didn't greet you in its finished state, but we're getting there. Susan Blackburn is actually a bit ahead of schedule, but I'm sure something will go wrong to correct that."

"May I inquire about the origins of your title?" Stone asked.

"Oh, that arrived some thirty-odd years ago, at a time when I was giving rather too much money to the Conservative Party. Margaret Thatcher, who was a good friend, saw to it."

"Somehow, I had thought it more ancient."

"Like me, you mean?"

Stone smiled. "Hardly."

The steward appeared and announced dinner.

They dined in the Members Dining Room, the only people there, and they were surrounded by portraits of former commodores of the Squadron, gazing down on them, some of whom were kings. The conversation flowed freely.

"It's nice that we have the place to ourselves," Sir Charles said, when their dishes had been taken away, to be replaced by port and Stilton. "It will be crowded at the weekend, and I'm happy to have had the opportunity to get to know you, Stone."

"Stone was very impressed with your property, Charles," Felicity said.

"Particularly the airfield," Stone said. He took

his checkbook from his pocket and tore out one, already filled out. He signed it and handed it to Sir Charles. "I believe that is the correct amount?" he said.

Sir Charles put on his glasses and read the check carefully. "We have the same bank," he said, tucking the check into a pocket and offering his hand.

Stone shook it. "Please give me a week to move the funds from New York."

"Of course."

"In the meantime, a member of my law firm's London office will be in touch with your solicitor to prepare the necessary documents."

Sir Charles handed him two business cards. "One is mine, the other, my solicitors'. Will you be able to stay for the completion?"

"I'll call my office and see if they can spare me," Stone said.

They drank their port, then Sir Charles changed back into his suit, and they returned to Felicity's boat. There was still a little light in the sky when they dropped off Sir Charles at his dock.

"Do you ride, Stone?" Bourne asked.

"Yes, Charles."

"Then why don't you wander over tomorrow morning, and I'll give you a tour of the property on horseback. Stay for lunch."

"I'd like that very much," Stone said, "but I don't have the clothes."

"I can help you with that," Felicity said.

"Ten o'clock, then?"

"I'll look forward to it."

They continued to Felicity's dock.

"That went awfully well," Felicity said as they walked up the path to her cottage. "Just as it should have gone."

"I am absolutely thrilled," Stone said. "Thank you so much for arranging everything so beautifully."

Then they went upstairs and went to bed, something to which they had both been looking forward.

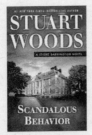
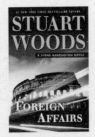